*To: Mac
Happy
Happy Reading !
Enjoy the Adventure!!*

Winnie and the Mystery of the Missing Moonstones

THE TROLL SERIES—VOLUME ONE

by

JP Coman

*J. Coman
P Coman*

Illustrated by

Maïlys Pitcher

Crimson Dragon Publishing
Aurora Colorado

Crimson Dragon Publishing
4255 S Buckley Rd, #405
Aurora, Colorado 80013-2951

www.crimsondragonpublishing.com

contact: Dawn Clark
dawn@crimsondragonpublishing.com
720-231-5646

Acknowledgements

To Bud and Cathy, and to Brenda, for thorough reading, editing, and honest comments.

To friends in the Midland West Texas Writer's group who encouraged me.

To my sister Patricia who encouraged me and made some important suggestions.

To David and Julie, two of my children who helped me reach for excellence.

To Dawn Clark, my editor, for helping me make the book even better.

To Beta Readers Diane, Brittany, Jen and Stella

To my wife, Phyllis, who developed the story with me and never let me get away with insufficient motivation or characters. This book started out as a screenplay, "The Troll Movie" in 1992.

Dedication

The book is gratefully dedicated to my youngest daughter, Julie. In the back of the Ford Van, returning from another long West Texas weekend away, playing with her troll dolls, Julie said, "I don't believe in Humans. Humans aren't real." And that was the genesis of the whole story.

Winnie and the Mystery of the Missing Moonstones

Volume One of The Troll Series

JP Coman

Illustrated by Mailys Pitcher

Chapter 1
Once Upon a Bridge

It all started with a trip to Pine Texas State Forest when I was 11. The forest and campgrounds are somewhere east of Dallas. My brother Jerry said we drove five thousand two hundred and eighty feet, which is stupid. I'm only a year younger than he is and I know how long a mile is. But it was a really long drive in Dad's SUV. Mom stayed home because she had a women's ministry meeting that Saturday. I could have stayed with my friend Beka at her house, but no, Dad said I had to go *fishing* and *camping.*

Going on an overnight with the Girl Scouts is one thing but camping for a whole weekend with my Dad and my aggravating brother is another. "Dad, why can't we stay at the Holiday Inn? What's wrong with a nice bathroom and a bed? Who cares about camping?"

Dad said, "Winnie, camping is more fun than theme parks." Now that's the most ridiculous statement in the history of the world, because NOTHING is more fun than theme parks. I mean, you get a whole day at the park, snack when you feel like it, ride the rides as many times as you want, and watch about a million people.

So, Dad was driving the SUV, maps and papers in the front seat, and Jerry and I were in the back seat. Jerry made me sit behind Dad so he couldn't see me, and Jerry could just look innocent for Dad.

The road was curvier than I expected. Dad is so impossible, in a funny kind of way, because he wouldn't use his cell phone for directions. He makes pronouncements like, "No Distracted Driving" even for the GPS app on his phone. I wasn't using my phone either, but Jerry was.

Jerry said, "Dad, my Map says this isn't the way to Pine State Forest."

"I know a better way! My friend, Julius Johnson..."

I said, "Officer Johnson?"

"Yes, that's right. You know him, he knows all the back ways to avoid all the traffic and the crowds."

So, we were driving the back roads in the wrong direction, and not a Holiday Inn to be seen. I was trying to arrange my stuff. Binky, my purple hair troll doll is probably my favorite because of the little shiny gemstone she has over her heart. My other dolls don't have such a nice one. I wanted to put the scout leader outfit on Binky, so I took off the police uniform, and when I put the doll down, Jerry grabbed it.

"Hey, give me that back!" I yelled.

"Come and get it," he said.

"Dad!" I called.

Dad kept looking from the map to the road, and back to the map. There was no way he could see the road, but here we go, as if Dad knew exactly what he was doing.

"There's a signpost. Ah, seven miles. ALL

RIGHT! We'll be there before night."

"That's what you said the last time," said Jerry. "And we're still lost. Why don't you use the CB radio?"

"Ha! Who needs it? We're practically there," Dad said.

I grabbed Jerry's music player so he would give me my troll back.

"Hey, give that back," he said.

"Give me Binky first".

"You have a hundred of these. You won't miss this one." Jerry was playing with Binky in the window—the OPEN WINDOW–on his side of the car, singing these stupid made up songs.

Oh, I'm going for a stroll, La La La
Cause I'm a little Troll, Ha Ha Ha
I'm really very old, Ga Ga Ga!

I unbuckled my seat belt and tried to get Binky.

"Come on, stop that. Be careful. Give it back to me," I said.

We were obviously bothering Dad. "We're

really close now kids." Then he glanced back. "Jerry close the window."

I couldn't believe it. Jerry closed the window just enough so that the doll was held between the glass and the frame, stuck there by the power window. And Jerry kept on singing.

I'm so strong and bold, Ra Ra Ra.
I'm never gonna fold, Ya Ya Ya
It's getting very cold, Wa Wa Wa.

I was SO mad. "Stop it, Jerry, before he falls out! Give it!"

Dad was mad then, too. "Winnie, keep it down. Jerry stop aggravating her."

Then we almost died.

On the bridge the car swerved and hit the curb on my side. I thought for sure we were going off the road down the steepest hill I had ever seen. Then as Dad struggled to recover, the car hit the curb on Jerry's side, and Binky fell out of the car window into the ravine. I was reaching for it, and without my seat belt on, I fell against Jerry. For a second, I thought

I was going to fall out the door after the doll. I screamed.

Dad got control of the car again and stopped just on the other side of the bridge.

"Winnie, keep quiet! Look what you two made me do. I can't believe it! You're not buckled in!"

Jerry chose that moment to be Mister Innocent. "I didn't do anything."

"He threw my doll out the window," I said.

"It wanted some fresh air," said Jerry.

"It did not!" I said, as I threw open the car door.

"Hold it," Dad said. "What are you doing? Close your door."

"My doll. It fell out the window," I said. "Thanks to him."

"Look, the doll is lost. That ravine goes all the way to the valley floor. Nobody can climb it. Be sure your door is closed and locked and buckle your seat belts. We're almost there."

So that's how I lost Binky. I couldn't believe Jerry could be so mean. I couldn't believe Dad wouldn't let me look for my doll. And I couldn't believe that this stupid trip was starting out this badly.

I wondered what happened to Binky.

Chapter 2
The Discovery

Oola and Humphrey heard the sounds of something falling from above the valley floor. Humphrey heard it first, the tipping of the branches and leaves. Falling things make a specific sound that Humphrey knew, and this was a falling thing, not a climbing thing or a crawling thing. Neither Humphrey nor Oola actually saw it fall, but the thud it made on the ground just beyond was clear enough.

"What was that?" said Oola.

"It sure wasn't an acorn," said Humphrey.

They peeked out from the branches. Oola peeked first, her sun-lightened amber hair forming a dip above her head. Then Humphrey, with his wild lime green strands that seemed to go in every direction, peeked next. Humphrey saw it in the dirt face down. "It's a troll!"

"Poor fellow, he's down," said Oola.

"Let's go!" said Humphrey.

Oola and Humphrey stepped closer to the troll on the ground. Oola spoke out. "Hey, are you okay? Hey."

Humphrey said, "Hey, buddy, wake up. Wake up, friend."

Humphrey touched the troll with the purple hair and recoiled in horror. That scared Oola, and they both backed up a few steps.

"What's the matter?" asked Oola.

"He's cold. He's so stiff. Oh, I touched him," cried Humphrey. "What are we going to do, Oola?"

"We'd better do something. If one of those rattlesnakes gets a taste of him, they might come looking for us next," said Oola.

"Oh, no! Rattlesnakes! Maybe he's already been bitten. Maybe the snake is already looking for seconds. Maybe he's told other snakes. Maybe all the snakes are looking for us."

"Well, listen for snakes," said Oola.

"I can't hear them. My ears are failing. It's getting dark! My eyes are going too," said Humphrey.

Oola grabbed Humphrey by the shoulders and put her face right in front of him.

"HUMPHREY! Look at me. Can you see me?"

"Well, of course I can see you, Oola."

Then Oola whispered, "Can you hear me, too?"

Humphrey looked confused and looked around and then back at Oola. "Yes, I can hear you. Why are we whispering?"

"To show you, your ears are FINE!"

Oola led Humphrey back to the troll. Oola bent down and took a tentative touch. Humphrey shivered, but Oola girded her strength and lifted the troll. She was surprised how light it was and dropped it right away.

"What's the matter?" asked Humphrey. "What is it? Is he alive?"

"This isn't a troll."

"What is it? A dwarf? An elf? A pixie?

"It's a doll," said Oola.

"A doll shaped like a full-grown troll?"

"It's made of rubber or something." Oola turned the doll face up and saw the plastic jewel. She gasped in surprise. "Look, a moonstone!"

Humphrey rushed to look but squinted his eyes at the jewel. "That's not a moonstone. It's a fake. It's like glass. It's a bauble."

"What's a bauble?" asked Oola.

"It's a fake glass moonstone, that's what it is. It hardly shines at all, and it's not sparkly, and its junk. Too bad, too. I wish it had been a moonstone."

Suddenly, Oola was excited. "Let's bring it to Mayfield and show everybody."

Humphrey was confused. "The bauble?"

"No, silly. The doll"

Humphrey put his hands on his hips. "What for? What is everyone going to do with this dumb doll?"

Oola moved to the side of the doll. "It'll be fun. Come on. You pick up that side, and I'll get this side."

Oola and Humphrey lifted the doll and began walking. "I think they will care more about the bauble," said Humphrey.

Chapter 3
The Deserted Camp

Dad really thought he had everything under control. He thought we didn't see anything unusual in the Ranger check-in station. So what if there were no other cars or RVs in the park. So what if the sign said, "Open April through September" and it was October 3rd. Dad thought we were just going to believe anything and everything he said.

Jerry was throwing the football with me. That's how bored I was; I was actually throwing it back. When Dad returned, Jerry went up to him. "Dad, this place is deserted," he said as he got back into the car.

"It's spooky," I said.

Dad had an answer for everything. "That's the

beauty of it. Just us and nature. No other noisy campers to bother us. The Ranger said they usually don't get campers this weekend." Then Dad turned red because he realized he didn't mean to say this.

Jerry caught it right away. "Wasn't he expecting us?"

I said, "Didn't you mail the reservations?"

Then my brilliant Dad, a Captain in the Dallas police force, turned an envelope on the front seat face down, as if we just didn't see it at all. "Sure, sure. Of course, I did. But, ah, the ranger said this is a very light weekend. We should have lots of fun."

We started seeing the campground signs:

POOL CLOSED

TENNIS COURT CLOSED

NO RUNNING

NO FISHING

NO SWIMMING

NO FOOTBALL THROWING

NO CAMPFIRES

Now I was really upset. This trip was going downhill fast. Binky was gone. The camp was a ghost town. And no campfires? "Dad, how can we have a marshmallow roast without campfires?"

"They mean no unauthorized campfires. I have a permit right here. Cost me ten bucks."

So, we drove down the hill, looking for this one particular campsite that's practically at the bottom of the world. I mean, the whole place was empty, right? And we had to find this one spot, and the lower we went, the darker it got. And we finally saw the tiny, broken sign that said, "115", so Dad pulled in and turned off the car.

It got suddenly quiet, like my ears quit working. I couldn't hear anyone breathing. We stepped out of the car, and for some reason, nobody said anything. There didn't seem to be any crickets, or birds, or tree frogs, or any other sounds except—except nothing. We were standing right in front of the car when "BAM" the car made a huge explosive hissing sound, and everyone screamed. I thought my heart was going to jump out of my throat.

I screamed, "What was that?"

Dad said, "Calm down, I think it's the radiator."

Jerry said, "Oh, great. Now we're really stuck here."

I couldn't believe it. If this was a reality TV show, it would be "Camp Irony".

Dad said, "Tomorrow I'll look at the problem, and if I can't fix it, I'll hike up to the Ranger station and get a ride into town to see about it."

We didn't know then, but at that very moment, the Ranger was locking up the Station and putting up a sign that read:

CAMPGROUND SERVICES

CLOSED UNTIL APRIL 1

Chapter 4
Mayfield

The troll village of Mayfield was having a festival. Trolls of every size and shape, with hair colors of every possible tint and hue, were watching two wrestling trolls dressed in colorful shorts. A referee stood by watching closely in his black-and-white striped tunic, and his black-and-gray striped hair.

Oola and Humphrey marched into town on the main path, carrying the purple-hair doll between them.

At first, only a few townspeople noticed. But awareness grew quickly, and the cheers of the crowd died down, replaced by gasps and whispers. Gunter, the wrestling troll in blue, had his back to Oola and Humphrey. He didn't see them walk into town. Wanjo, in a red outfit, looked up at Oola and Humphrey and was distracted. Gunter took advantage and tackled Wanjo, but the referee didn't call a foul, because he, too, was looking at the doll. Finally, Gunter saw what everyone else saw.

Of course, everyone knew Oola, the happy troll with yellow hair in a tan tunic with a sash around her waist. And everyone knew Humphrey, the sensitive troll with green hair in a leafy coverall that had no shape at all. But no one had ever seen the stiff, pale purple-hair troll doll with a shiny jewel.

Merkle, a short and talkative troll with an orange tunic and orange hair, had a lot to say about the crowd that was forming around the troll doll. Actually, Merkle usually had a lot to say. In fact, Merkle always had a lot to say about everything.

"I don't know what that is, but I don't think it is a good idea for you to bring that thing here. What is it? Is it some kind of fairy? I hope not because fairies are so scary because they fly and wave their arms and glow at night and all—but this doesn't look like a fairy so it must be an ogre. Oh my gosh OOLIE and HUMP brought an ogre into Mayfield! I wonder if it's dead. They're carrying it like a big stick or something like it's just a piece of wood."

While Merkle was talking, Mayor Omudu of Mayfield approached Oola, Humphrey, and the doll. The townspeople were still giving the doll a wide berth and looking without touching as best they could.

Omudu said, "Oola, Humphrey, tell us about your friend."

"We found it..." said Oola.

"...face down," said Humphrey.

"...in the Southern Passage by..."

"...it was just like this, all stiff and full of..." Humphrey stopped talking when Oola gave him a look.

"Go on. You tell the story," said Oola.

Humphrey looked down at his big feet and said, "No, you tell it."

Mayor Omudu said, "And what do you make of that?" indicating the jewel.

Humphrey regained his enthusiasm. "Oh, it's

not really a moonstone. It's fake glass, that's what it is. It's a bauble. It's not real."

Mayor Omudu touched the doll once and then put his hand down. The crowd was very still, waiting and wondering what Mayor Omudu would say. Next to him stood Asa, the oldest female troll in the village, not counting her mother, Aerona. Their family were considered to be the wisest, also, and sometimes Mayor Omudu's pronouncements were simply echoes of Asa's. Just when it seemed that the Mayor was going to tell everyone what he thought, Merkle interrupted.

"How do you know it's not real, Humphrey? Did you try it yet? Did you wish on it? Because it might be a moonstone. I never saw a moonstone before, but that might be one."

The Mayor tried to be patient with him. "Young Merkle, Humphrey is right. This is not a real moonstone. There haven't been any moonstones in our village for many years." He said this part with a sadness that all the older trolls understood.

Merkle was not satisfied. "Well, you didn't

try either. What if it's a real moonstone on this thing? What if it was given to us by some... some human?" The crowd roared with laughter. They were used to Merkle saying things that were out of the ordinary, and unexpected. But this took everyone completely by surprise and relieved the tension.

"That's ridiculous, Merkle," said Mayor Omudu. "Humans aren't real. They're just stories. Didn't your mother tell you that?"

"Well, everyone says they're just stories," replied Merkle, "but maybe they're true. I think they're true. Whenever someone tells a human story, I always get real scared and all. How come trolls always tell human stories if they're not real?"

Asa's strong, clear voice interrupted Merkle. "It is a sacrilege."

The crowd reacted to this with gasps and nods, and everyone seemed to step back a bit. Mayor Omudu spoke. "Asa is correct. I find the thing repulsive. Remove it from our village, and send it over the waterfalls, never to return. Take the hare and the fox with you, for luck and protection."

As soon as the Mayor finished speaking, a rabbit and a fox appeared, coming out of the deep green hedge growth. They stood obediently nearby, waiting. No one approached them to pet them or speak to them, because they knew these animals were "on duty."

Oola looked at Humphrey. "Come on, Humphrey. We have an important job to do."

Humphrey had a very scared expression on his face. But he realized that he found the doll, and now he had to get rid of it. "OK. I can't stand to look at that bauble anymore, anyway."

Mayor Omudu spoke to the crowds. "None of you will speak of this thing again." Then he left the town square, going into the hut that was his town hall. The crowd also dispersed, except for a few who watched Humphrey and Oola carry the doll, followed by the hare and the fox.

Merkle also watched, and continued talking, as was his custom, to everyone and no one. "A sacrilege. Did you hear what Asa and Mayor Omudu said? That thing is a sacrilege. I've never seen a sacrilege before, but that's one.

I would have known right away that it was a
sacrilege if I had been the one to find it, because
if I would have been on the Southern passage
and had seen that thing, I'd have known that's
what it was because it looks like a sacrilege. It
doesn't look like a troll at all, with those buggy
eyes and that stick-up hair and no clothes and
all stiff like that. I'd have known right away."

****

The waterfall was at the Eastern edge of the land that the trolls lived in. None of the trolls ever explored beyond that area, because there really was no need. The trolls had everything they needed near Mayfield. So there was a certain fascination, even fear about the waterfalls. And to these two trolls, the waterfalls were about the most fearsome thing they had ever encountered.

Oola and Humphrey had to climb a tree with the doll and drop it from a branch directly over the crashing water. The two trolls, individually, were strong enough and agile enough to climb a tree, but they had never attempted to haul a big life-sized doll with them. It took them a couple of attempts to figure out how to do it. Oola climbed to the first limb, and Humphrey lifted the doll to her, and then he climbed up after to allow her to climb higher and take the doll to the next level.

Finally, Oola was sitting on the limb that would take them out over the water. Humphrey was near the trunk, and the doll was between them.

Oola said, "Hump, come on. We're almost there."

"I'm going to fall in!" said Humphrey, frightened.

"No, you're not. Help me move it over the water."

"I can't let go."

"Sure you can, just for a second. Just push the doll a little towards me so I can reach it."

Humphrey tried to lift his hand and take the doll, but then grabbed the limb again. He steadied himself, and tried again, but his hand shot back to the limb for support. Oola realized that he might not ever get the doll over to her, so she began to move just an inch or two back to Humphrey. It was at that moment that Humphrey got his balance enough to pick up the doll with his free hand and move it towards Oola. She didn't expect the doll to be moving, and it hit her just enough to cause her to lose her balance.

"Oohh, wait!" cried Oola. She threw her arm around searching for balance.

"Hold on!"

"I'm trying," said Oola, as her legs started getting wobbly.

"Be careful,".

"Aaah!" cried Oola, as she lost her balance completely. Oola and the doll fell off the tree limb and plummeted down into the waterfall.

Humphrey watched, trying to find them in the great white plumes of foam as the water

roared and crashed. He scampered down the tree much faster than he had climbed it and began calling out from the river's edge.

"Oola? Oola! Where are you? Are you OK?"

* * *

At sunset, Humphrey burst into the town square from the forest path. Merkle was the first to see him.

"Humphrey is back, but where is Oola? What's going on? The hare and fox came back with him. Did you get rid of the sacrilege?"

As Humphrey approached the town hall hut, Omudu came out to meet him. Humphrey spoke right away. "Oola's gone." Humphrey's tears began flowing freely. "She fell into the great waterfall, and it's all my fault."

The town trolls quickly gathered around to hear Humphrey's story.

"We were standing on the tree limb, above the water, when it happened so fast. She moved, and I moved, and the doll was in the way, and suddenly, there they went, the doll and Oola, falling into the great water. I looked and looked for her. I called and called, and the hare sniffed, and the fox looked, but we couldn't find her. She's gone."

The trolls of the town cried, and hugged, and gave their support to Humphrey, and began to disperse. Humphrey was left in the square, sitting at the fountain wall, when Asa approached, as quietly as ever.

"Young troll, with eyes of the hawk and ears of the fawn, you are very brave and true."

"But, Asa, it's all my fault."

"No! Listen." Asa began to whisper, but with a very glad, almost giggly tone. "Oola lives. She has not perished. I would know it. I would feel it."

"But she fell...into the waterfall."

"But she did not die. You and I will go find her. She needs us. Come, we have a journey to make—together."

Chapter 5
The Campsite

I wanted to roast marshmallows. I mean, if there is one thing that camping is good for, it's roasting marshmallows. You can't do it at home even if you have a gas stove. We tried at my friend Julie's house, but all we did was make a mess and then it took hours to clean it up.

Now that I think about it, roasting marshmallows isn't really the thing that saves camping. It's the people around the campfire. When I was in Girl Scouts, we talked and sang, someone had a guitar, the fire was huge, and we made the best S'mores ever.

So here I was, in Dullsville State Forest, with my dear old-fashioned Dad, and Jerry who was eating marshmallows right out of the bag. We were roasting marshmallows on a tiny little fire with two skinny logs. We had to poke our marshmallows on the end of a stick and hold them over the fire.

"They won't let the fires be any bigger," explained Dad.

"It's okay," I said, because what else could I say.

"Hold your branch closer, honey."

Okay, Dad knows best, so I moved my stick into the fire. He practically jumped up to correct me. "No, closer to you, away from the fire." Right then, my marshmallow melted off the stick and dropped into the fire. And all Dad could say was, "Oh, look. See?"

I was going to take this as just another stupid thing about this campground, but the Jerk started laughing. And laughing. And falling off his camp stool, and snickering.

"Stop it." I said.

But he kept on laughing. He held up the crumpled plastic bag and said, "Last one!" He took the last marshmallow from the bag and held it up, and I am so dumb I thought he was handing it to me. I reached over and was about to say, "Thanks," when he shoved it into his mouth, and almost gagged laughing.

"Jerry!" I threw my stick at him, and he just laughed harder. "Stop it, you jerk. Just shut up!"

Dad said, "Now, honey, don't throw the stick. You might have burned him."

I screamed, "I wish I HAD." I had to get out of there, so I just ran, not caring about the darkness, not caring about the snakes, or the stream, or anything. It was so not fair. I only wanted to do ONE THING on this stupid waste of time camping trip, and Jerry had just ruined it.

I found the drop-off to the stream sooner than I expected. My foot slipped, and my hands got all scratched up when I grabbed the trees. I ended up almost falling into the stream completely, nose to the water's edge, muddy and bruised.

I wanted to scream. But I didn't because then Dad and Jerry would come and laugh at me. I did the only thing I could do, just lay there. I put my hands on the soft muddy bank, and put my chin on my hands, and just watched the water from a crocodile's point of view. "Wait a minute," I said to myself. "What if there are crocodiles?" I listened a little harder, but there were no crocodile sounds, or if there were, I didn't recognize them.

My eyes were adjusted pretty well to the darkness now, and even though there was only a quarter moon, I could still see things. I could make out things floating by in the water. There was a stick. Then a little turtle head, which was pretty neat. Then there was—what? I could make out a nose, a belly, and two feet. My eyes opened wide.

"Binky?" I didn't expect my troll to answer me, but I was just too astonished. Was this real? I got up, leaned over the bank, and found I couldn't reach it. I was going to miss if I didn't get it right away. I took a step into the water and almost jumped right out again, it was so cold. But Binky was already past me, so I took two more quick steps, and grabbed it.

As cold as the water was, this was my chance to get the mud off of me, so I quickly splashed a little water on my jeans and my shirt, and got even colder. I was just about to get out of the water onto the bank, when I saw another floating object in the stream. It looked like another troll doll; it had a nose, a belly, and two feet. I grabbed it and climbed back to the bank and plopped down on the ground.

"Okay, you're Binky," I said aloud. I looked at the second troll. "Two trolls! Jerry, you Jerk." He must have tossed two of my dolls out the window. But this second doll didn't have a gemstone. And the hair was plastered down its face, so it was hard to see which of my dolls it was.

I started moving the hair out of its face, when its eyes popped open, and looked right back at me. That's when I screamed and dropped both Binky and this—this other thing on the ground. I jumped back, breathing hard.

Perhaps it was a trick of the moonlight, I thought. Of course. Now I felt really dumb. I looked again. Yep, just a toy.

The troll sat up and rubbed its eyes. Then it coughed.

I started shaking.

It looked at Binky on the ground next to it. Then it actually stood up!

The troll looked right at me and screamed. "Aaahhh! A Human!"

And I screamed, "Aaahhh! A Troll!" I ran behind a tree, and it ran behind a tree, and we waited.

I looked again, and saw the troll peering around the tree, looking at me.

"Are you a real live troll?" I asked stupidly.

"Are you a real live human?"

"Yes, but trolls aren't really alive."

"Human's aren't real, but trolls are," it answered.

This was a girl troll. "What's your name?"

"What's yours?" the troll asked.

"Winnie."

"I'm Oola."

"I didn't think trolls were really real."

"Then what's this? I'll bet it's yours."

"That's Binky. It's just a doll. I thought real trolls would be mean and ugly."

"You're thinking of ogres. I thought that real humans would be mean and ugly."

"You're thinking of big brothers. They're not human."

Oola put her hand on top of her head and lifted the strands of her hair. "Oh, my hair. I must look terrible."

"You look like a frog, all wet and shiny."

Oola looked like she was going to cry at this.

So, I said, "Oh, I'm sorry. I must look like a pig, with all this mud and everything."

Oola looked at the stream, and then at me. "I think you saved my life."

"I did?"

"I will repay my debt to you. What would you like? I will give you whatever I can."

I remembered how everything went bad today. "I want to go home and forget all about this stupid camping trip. Can you do that?"

Oola looked down at her feet. "No. I cannot. Trolls do not have this power without our moonstones."

I was kind of embarrassed that I put her on the spot like that. "Oh, I'm sorry. I didn't know." I moved a little closer to her and picked up my troll doll. "Do you want to use Binky's?"

Oola looked very annoyed at me. "That is not a moonstone. That is a bauble."

Now I was really confused, but I wanted to make her feel better. "Oh, well, maybe I don't want to go home just yet. I just wish..."

"Yes?" she said, expectantly.

"Well, I really wanted to roast marshmallows

at our campfire with my Dad, but my stupid brother ate them all."

At this, Oola's eyes opened wide. "I love marshmallows!"

"You do?"

Oola started hopping about. "Come on, let's go!"

"Where?"

"To your campfire!"

"All right!" I said and started back to the camp. When I got to the top of the riverbank, I looked back, and Oola was struggling to get up the steep slope.

"I'm coming," she said, but it was hopeless.

"You can't keep up." I said, trying not to be cruel.

"Wow, are you fast!"

"Yeah, I guess so. I guess I should carry you. What do you think?"

"C-c-carry me?" said Oola.

"Well, I did pluck you out of the water. I guess I've already carried you once."

She straightened up and looked up at me. "That's right. You're Winnie, the ... human who saved my life."

I put Binky into my hip pocket and bent down. "Are you ready, Oola? I don't want to squish you."

Oola almost cried. "Why'd you have to say that?"

"Sorry. Here." I put my hand down on the grass, and Oola stepped on it. She was about six inches tall, and even though I had carried her before, it wasn't the same. Before, I thought she was just a doll, and it didn't matter how hard I squeezed a doll. Now she was a real live troll, and I was very careful. I cupped my hands around her and walked slowly.

"The camp is this way." I said.

Oola looked around. "I've never been here before."

Chapter 6
Marshmallow Rain

"Winnie!"

I heard my dad calling. Oola was suddenly trying to wriggle out of my hands.

"Put me down!" Oola was insisting. "Put me down here."

I put her down in the grass. "But, what about the marshmallows? ... Oola?"

But Oola didn't say anything. She just scampered away. I was amazed how quickly she disappeared into the grasses and woods. But it was still quite dark. A cloud was beginning to cover the moon, and I got turned around in my directions.

"Dad. I'm coming. Where are you?

"Over here."

I found the camp, but I was so disappointed Oola had broken her promise. I sat down by the fire, and I wanted to tell Dad about Oola, but I knew he wouldn't understand. Dad, on the other hand, had plenty to say: about leaving the campsite when it was so late, about getting muddy and wet, about not coming back when he called. As he went on and on, for the first time, I could actually hear the "blah, blah, blah" in Dad's voice.

* * *

Oola did not run away. She began looking carefully for certain leaves and roots of a few special plants that she knew about. She gathered them into a little pile, stopped, sniffed, and looked up a tree. There was a honeycomb far up in the trunk, out of reach. Oola called up to the nest, "Honeybee!"

A guardian bee came out immediately and buzzed down and around Oola. She looked at it flying around her.

"Ooh, you are a big strong guard bee!"

The bee buzzed around her a little closer.

Oola followed it by turning around.

"Honeybee, bring me a bit of fresh honeycomb from your nest."

The honeybee obeyed immediately and returned with a hexagon-shaped piece from the comb. It dropped the honey and Oola caught it.

Oola then pulled a leaf off a nearby bush and spread it like a tablecloth over the ground. She put the honey and some ground up bits of root on the leaf and worked them together. Then she took a bamboo straw, placed one end into the mixture, placed the other end into her mouth, and began to blow. A white puffy shape began to form. Oola smiled.

***

My dad finally finished his lecture and told us to get our sleeping bags ready for bed. He entered the tent and started changing for bed. Jerry came up close to me whispering so Dad wouldn't hear, "Too bad you found your way back."

I just shook off his words. Then Jerry tried again.

"You will note, we DIDN'T go looking for you."

I turned and slapped Jerry as hard as I could, but only ended up hurting my hand on his shoulder. I was so angry. "And you had to go and eat all the marshmallows."

Suddenly a marshmallow fell in front of us. I looked at it in the dust at our feet, then I looked at Jerry to see if he was doing something weird. Then I looked up and dozens of marshmallows began raining down upon us. I gasped and caught some.

Jerry was astonished. "What? What's going on? Marshmallows?" Jerry, cautious at first, finally started catching some. More were falling from the trees.

I was so excited. "They are! They're round marshmallows!"

"And they're golden. Round, golden marshmallows!"

Finally, I spied Oola in a tree, tossing the last marshmallow to me and winking. I grinned and waved back. Oola lost her footing and had to grab onto a limb to keep from falling right

out of the tree.

Dad emerged from the tent just then, barefoot and wearing loud striped red and yellow pajamas, and stepped on a marshmallow. "Oh, no! What a mess! Look at this. We're going to have ants and flies, and..."

Jerry interrupted. "Dad, you should've seen it! It was raining marshmallows!"

"Don't give me that, young man."

"Honest! It's true," said Jerry. "Ask her! They were just falling down from the trees or something."

"Now you pick each one of these up and get them to the trash. You know better than to mess up this campsite. I can't believe it. What a mess."

Now Jerry looked sheepish and asked me for help.

"Win! Tell him."

Jerry looked from me to Dad, but Dad didn't wait for an answer. He ducked back inside the tent.

I finally got the last word in. "Raining marshmallows. Right." I smiled, put a single marshmallow on to a stick, and began roasting it.

Chapter 7
Go Fish

I awoke the next morning to the wonderful aroma of a hot breakfast. And I was totally surprised that I had slept so well the night before, with all the excitement. But when I got dressed and looked around, I didn't see Oola anywhere. I understand that she didn't just want to run out in front of Dad and Jerry and say, "Hi there, I'm a real live troll!" But she didn't have to hide from me.

There was a constant droning noise in the back of my head. It was Dad, talking non-stop about the day's activities.

"The radiator problem was a minor leak, so I fixed it. As for today's activities, we'll go fishing, and then a nice hike in the woods before it's too hot. We'll have lunch and go for a swim in the lake. There are rental canoes, and I brought horseshoes. Then we'll make a nice fire and for supper we'll cook all the fish we've caught."

Jerry looked at me and said, "The fish are looking forward to this." Then he said, "Dad, I've never seen you catch a fish in my whole life."

"Oh, so you think I'm out of my element? Like I'm just a city guy? I've been fishing a few times in my life, let me tell you."

Dad proceeded to tell him. I just looked at the sky and the trees, and then I saw her. Oola was standing on a branch, and when she caught my eye, she waved and almost fell off the branch. I laughed.

"You don't believe me, Winnie?" asked my Dad.

I looked at him carefully to see if he saw me looking at Oola, but he didn't. I picked up Binky and said to him, "Dad, rubbing a troll's hair brings you good luck."

Jerry looked at the troll doll, then at me and said, "Hey, isn't that the same doll that, uh, fell out the window?"

Dad looked at Binky said, "Oh, for heaven's sake, Winnie."

Jerry was still stammering, "Where did you...? How did you find...?"

I kept holding my doll out, then Dad said, "Oh, well, it can't hurt." He reached out and rubbed Binky's hair. "There."

That was, I think, the first time my Dad ever touched one of my dolls. I'm going to have to post this to my feed when I get reception – the phone still says *No Service*.

After breakfast, we headed to the pond. The fishing pier was kind of old and rickety. It didn't seem safe to stand on, but we managed.

Fishing seemed to bring out the hillbilly in my dad. He began to drawl in a country accent. "Back at the park entrance, the Ranger told me about the legend of Ol' Blue. People have been trying to catch Ol' Blue now for nigh on to thirteen years. Ol' Blue is the biggest, orneriest, sneakiest, and fastest smallmouth bass in the hill country."

Jerry might be fooled, but I thought I knew

better. I said, "There's no such thing. You're just making that up."

"It's what the Ranger told me. He said the closest he had come to catching Ol' Blue himself was one evening about two years ago. He had brought some fresh jumbo shrimp to see if Blue had an appetite for them. Well, when most of his bait had been taken, he figured that was that, but then, on the last shrimp, he got a bite, and it was a big one."

Jerry was, shall we say, hooked. "Wow! Was it Ol' Blue?"

There was no stopping Dad now. "That's the way the Ranger figured it. He said the fishing line just took off in his hands like lightning, and it took all his strength to hold on. The fish was swimming this way and that, and the Ranger was holding on for dear life, when his old worn out fishing rod broke and the reel and all went *kersplash* into the water. He said he's going to come out one day with all new equipment and try again."

What happened next made me wonder if Oola had a trick or two up her troll hair.

Suddenly, Jerry's fishing line took off, and the reel was spinning. "It's HIM!" Jerry screamed. He seemed astonished, joyful, and worried all at once.

"Hold on to him, Jerry. Reel him in, nice and easy. Don't jerk it." Dad was enjoying this just as much as Jerry.

Instead of the fish getting closer, it took off away from the pier like a speedboat. Dad moved behind Jerry, both of them holding on to the rod and reel.

"I'm losing it. He's getting away!" cried Jerry. Dad set his feet firmer on the pier and held on even tighter.

Just then, there was a strange sound, like a straining and a groaning. Then a loud popping and snapping sound. Jerry and Dad looked down at their feet, at the old creaky boards on the pier, and then they looked up at each other.

The pier broke off with a huge "Snap!" Instead of being thrown into the water, Jerry and Dad were pulled along like a waterski by what must have been the biggest fish in the world.

I finally found my voice. "Dad! Come back! What are you doing?"

The pier/ski/thing was moving so fast it was making a wake in the water behind it. Jerry and Dad were wet up to their knees, but still the thing kept moving. Then it stopped right in the middle of the pond, and they almost lost their balance on the floating piece of pier. It was ridiculous, seeing those two on a shaky, slippery broken off pier.

For a long moment, we all just kind of held our breath. Something wasn't right. I looked out to the pond…was that something moving in the water directly towards them?

Then one end of the pier flew up, and Dad and Jerry got dunked into the water. I laughed so hard it hurt.

"Dad! Jerry! Get out before you both get eaten. Hurry!"

Dad and Jerry half-swam, half-dragged themselves and the rod and reel to shore. We all looked back at the pond and a giant fish leaped into the air and splashed back down. Dad said, "How'd he get unhooked?" Dad seldom uses curse words, but I heard a few from him then, which I shall not repeat. At least, not here.

Chapter 8
The Cave

It wasn't my idea to try and put insect repellent on. If they had asked me, I would have said, "No way." Those sprays are so bad you can't shower off the smell for a week.

But Dad said, "This one smells good. Turn around," and sprayed my back and arms and legs, then he sprayed Jerry, then himself. "Gotta be careful about the mosquito virus, you know." Like my Dad knows.

It seemed like we had only been hiking for five minutes when we were swatting at mosquitoes right and left. Dad started reaching into his backpack, saying, "Let's put some more insect repellent on." That's when I got a good look at the can he was spraying us with.

"Dad, this isn't repellent. It's air freshener!"

Dad's eyes just about popped out, and he looked again at the can. "Oh no. We'll attract every bug for miles around."

We were jumping around swatting flies and mosquitoes like a clip you see in those funny video shows.

Jerry yelled, "Look!" Hundreds of birds were flying toward us.

"Run for your lives!" That was the first smart thing Jerry ever said. We started running down the path.

Dad yelled. "Hey, over here." We changed direction and followed him into a cave. The birds, thankfully, did not follow us.

I peeked out the entrance of the cave and saw birds snatching the bugs out of the air. A hummingbird came up and hovered right by my nose. Oola was riding on it! She stood up and waved, and then fell off the bird. Before she could fall to the ground, the hummingbird swooped down and allowed Oola to land on him. They flew off, Oola whooping and hollering with the tiniest voice.

I wanted to turn around and tell Dad and
Jerry to come and look because Oola was there.
Oola, a real live troll, not a doll. One that can do
all kinds of magical things. But when I looked
at them, they were just so caught up in the
weirdness, wondering about the insects, the
birds, and the cave.

I looked around and saw that something
had scratched up the wall. At first, I thought
it might be some huge animal sharpening its
claws on the rock. But the more I looked, the
more it seemed like a drawing. Then I noticed a
light at the back of the cave. Why is the back of
the cave lighter than where we were standing?
Maybe we could go out a different way.

"Guys, what's that light back there?" Both
Dad and Jerry turned to look.

"It's coming from somewhere up high," Dad
said.

"It's some kind of huge hole. I'll bet it goes up
a mile," Jerry said.

"Jerry, is there a mile-high mountain just
above our heads?" I said.

"OK, I was exaggerating." Jerry started to step

up on rocks to try and get into the hole.

"Uh, wait a minute, maybe you shouldn't go up there," Dad said. Maybe??? Of COURSE Jerry shouldn't be climbing up a hole in the back of a cave...

Suddenly the light went out. There was a strange flapping noise, then a strange screeching noise.

Then all the bats in the world started swooping down on us. We screamed and shook our heads and swatted the air and bumped into each other, and finally found the cave entrance and got out of there.

Chapter 9
The Bear

"The secret to horseshoes is absolute concentration."

Dad was totally in to this whole "family-time/quality-time/games" thing.

"Stand steady, feet placed five inches apart, left slightly in front of the right, knees bent..."

I was so tired of crazy fish, and mosquito raids, and bird attacks, and killer bats. Maybe there will be a wild forest animal to chase us back to civilization to escape this.

"...take a full backstroke with the shoe, and throw..."

As Dad was taking his best shot, a baby bear cub walked right into the edge of the clearing, on the other side of the makeshift horseshoe pit.

I said aloud, "Oh, look! How cute!"

That messed up Dad's absolute concentration, because he was in the middle of throwing the horseshoe.

He stammered. "What?" Dad's horseshoe flew wildly to a tree between the bear and us and hit a branch.

Jerry saw the bear cub too. "Hey there, little fella. Come here."

Dad said, "Don't touch it. This isn't the petting zoo. You kids be careful. That's a wild bear."

I said, "Oh, come on, Dad. It's just a cub. It wants to play."

The mother bear appeared, coming out of the trees and bushes at the edge of the clearing. Even though I saw the bear, it didn't register as dangerous at first. Here was a full-grown bear, sniffing the ground and coming directly toward me. But I didn't move. Part of me was thinking "OK, this is bad, this is very bad." But another part was, "I wasn't doing anything wrong. I didn't touch the cub. The bear is going to get

her cub and leave."

Dad and Jerry were behind me, yelling opposite warnings. "Don't move!" and "Run, Winnie!" and "Play 'dead'!" and "Throw a rock!"

The momma bear came closer on her hind legs, to where she was under the branch that the horseshoe hit. Something dropped down

from the branch, and the bear stopped. She
swatted at her ear, and then with a snort turned
around and left with her cub back into the
woods.

Dad and Jerry approached Winnie. "Win, are
you OK?"

Jerry said, "Wow, that was so cool. You are
the bravest little sister in the world. You looked
that old Mama bear right in the eye and stared
her down."

Both of them turned to look at where the
bear went. They tell me I fainted onto the grass.

Chapter 10
Meet the Troll

This whole camping vacation was such a contradiction. So much had gone so stupidly wrong, and yet, so many cool things had happened. I was tired, but also excited, because I thought I might see Oola again tonight. I kept looking at the branches of the trees above the campground, but she wasn't there.

Meanwhile, Dad was being Dad, trying to wring the most out of this trip. "Anyone for campfire songs?" He began singing "John Jacob Jingleheimer Schmidt!" at the top of his lungs. Jerry and I just kept quiet, and Dad, for a change, got the hint.

"Well, it's been a big day. While y'all were

resting, I put the extra gasoline into the tank, and the car's ready for us when we leave tomorrow. So, I guess I'll turn in."

Then Dad kissed us both and went into his tent. I counted to ten before the snoring started. I think that was a record for the fastest time from wake to sleep.

Jerry moved his chair closer to me and lowered his voice. "Win, you notice anything weird today?"

"Yeah. Dad's never been goofier."

"It's not just that. Something's going on."

"What do you mean?"

Jerry opened his mouth a couple of times, but then he frowned and seemed to forget the words. Then he spoke, slowly at first, and speeding up. "We barely caught any fish..."

"Hey, I caught seven!"

"OK, you caught fish, and Ol' Blue nearly drowned Dad and me. And those birds nearly attacked us when they came after the bugs... I felt like I was in a horror movie. And that bear! It didn't even touch you. Even when it was raining marshmallows, you seemed to be okay with it all. "

I could hardly contain my excitement. Jerry was treating me like a friend as well as a sister. Now was the perfect time, maybe the only time I could share my secret.

"Jer, you want to see what I found yesterday?"

Jerry looked at me sideways. "I don't know. What is it?"

I almost burst. "It's a troll! A real live troll!"

Jerry looked very confused. "Is this about the one that fell out of the car window? That IS the one you found… "

I realized he was on the wrong track. "Not Binky. A real troll and her name is Oola."

"Oola"

"Yes. Oola is a living troll. Not a doll."

Jerry didn't like that. "Sure, right."

I realized it was no good explaining it, there was only one thing I could do. "Oola, come out. Oola." I told Jerry, "She's been helping us all along."

Jerry started looking kind of scared. "Win, maybe you should lie down now. DAD!"

"Shh!" I said. "Don't wake up Dad. She's here.

Just listen."

Maybe I had been a bit too hasty, so I said very softly, "Ooooola."

I was looking at everything, but not really seeing anything. Jerry was looking around, more calm now. He probably thought I was still kidding, but he was going along with it. I rested my eyes on this one bush at the edge of the area and I saw two little feet under it. Jerry saw it too.

"It's just one of your dolls."

"Hush," I said to Jerry.

And then, Oola took a step forward and showed herself in the firelight. "Is he going to squish me?"

I realized I had described Jerry in unfavorable terms. "No, no, Jerry is not going to hurt you."

He watched Oola, standing there in the firelight, with her amber hair and yellow smock, looking back and forth at Jerry and me. Anyone could tell this was no doll, but a person, a very small, scared, living troll person.

Jerry freaked. "It's a trick! It's the campfire. I'm seeing shadows. It's the fumes. I'm breathing carbon monoxide. I'm seeing things. This is crazy. You're crazy. You've got me seeing little troll people that walk and talk and move and everything. Oh, no. Now I'm done for. I'm history. That's it. Pow! Ugh. I'm dead." And to prove it, he collapsed in the dust.

I reached down, stroking her long hair. She seemed to really like that.

"Jerry, just brush her hair. Then you'll be lucky like me."

Jerry opened one eye and said, "Is this a trick? Where are the batteries?"

He sat up and stared at the troll for a moment. "Wow." He realized it was true. Then he spoiled it. "Do magic for me."

Poor Oola looked at her feet. "I can't."

Jerry said, "A real troll can do magic."

Oola looked right at Jerry and said, "I AM a real troll. But," she took a breath, "I have no moonstone."

Jerry looked at me. "See, not a real troll. Can't do magic."

I was kind of confused too. "Oola, what about those fish I caught?"

Oola just giggled. "Fish are easy to fool."

Jerry said, "And then Ol' Blue showed up."

Oola got serious. "Well, that wasn't my idea."

I remembered seeing Oola on the hummingbird. "What about all those bugs; you brought the birds, didn't you?"

Oola laughed again. "The birds just came for the bugs."

Jerry said, "And then all those bats came and chased us out of the cave."

Oola frowned. "Well, that wasn't my idea either."

And then I remembered what I was trying to forget. "Hey, what about that bear?"

Jerry chimed in. "Yeah, that big old Mama bear?"

Oola stuck her little chin up in the air. "That definitely was not my idea! Moby just came by on her own. I wasn't the one fooling around with her baby cub. I could have broken my neck jumping from the branch onto her shoulders like that. I told Moby to stop and…"

And then she looked surprised. "I think I saved your life! Now the debt is paid. I can return to my village."

It hit me like a lightning bolt. "What? You're leaving? But Oola…"

Jerry said, "Hey, neat. I want to see the troll village."

Oola's eyes got big, and she put both her hands to her cheeks. "Oh, no. You may not follow."

Chapter 11
The Encounter

At that moment an ancient troll with white hair, wearing a long silver gown, stepped out from behind a bush, where I guess she had been listening to us. Another troll, a boy, came out right behind her.

Her voice was serious. "Indeed, you must not."

Oola exclaimed, "Asa!"

Even Jerry was pleased to see two more real live trolls. "Hey, cool. A troll convention."

Humphrey ran to Oola, saying, "Oolie, you really are alive! I was so scared for you. I looked and looked for you, but the water had taken you away."

Oola said, "It's okay, Humphrey."

Humphrey continued. "But Asa knew. She felt it. She knew you were alive."

Asa's commanding voice ended all the reunion chatter. "What Oola said earlier is right. The trolls in my village do not know about humans, except in dark stories. But you have befriended these, Oola."

Oola was quick to answer. "Winnie saved me from the stream. She saved my life."

Asa continued. "And I gather that you have returned the favor." Asa's countenance softened a little, and she smiled. "You have shown far more resourcefulness than I had seen, brave Oola."

Jerry interrupted Asa. "Say, can YOU do some magic?"

I couldn't believe he said it. "Jerry, stop that."

Asa's voice became very sharp. "Oola, did you tell these humans that you could perform magic?"

Oola shrank in fear. "Oh, no, Asa."

Asa then looked right at me. "Did she tell you why we cannot perform magic?"

I said simply, "She said you have no

moonstones."

Asa shocked everyone in the clearing with her next question. "Did she tell you there will soon be no more trolls?"

We all gasped at this. Asa moved closer to the campfire and sat down upon a branch, looking at the fire. Oola and I exchanged glances, and I was going to ask why, but Oola's look silenced me. Jerry and I sat down by the fire across from Asa. Oola and Humphrey sat alongside Asa, and everyone waited. After a long silence, Asa spoke.

"Long ago, every troll found her moonstone in the Brook of Truth, or near the Trees of Youth. It made her perpetually young, and unable to tell a lie. There were stones in the River of Courage and near the Rock of Strength. Trolls were peaceful rulers in the forest in those days, and all the animals gave heed to their bidding. Trolls were always fair and loving, so harmony was preserved."

Humphrey asked in a dreamy voice, not like his ordinary chattering, "What did the stones look like?"

Asa smiled and answered him. "Moonstones are beautiful, sparkly, special. They come in all the colors of the morning, deep and glowing. A troll found his moonstone on the first Spring day—just picked it out, like finding a flower. The moonstones helped us stay young, and trolls did not age. That is why trolls seem magical. To the very young the world is a magical place."

Jerry said, "So you're not gonna do magic?"

I punched him. "Hush!"

Asa said to Oola and Humphrey, "Did you

ever hear the song that young trolls sing when
going for their moonstones?"

Humphrey got excited and jumped up. "Oh,
yes, I remember!

"Every Springtime young trolls look
In Garden Grove and Babble Brook
We will find our special stone
One that's meant for us alone
One that makes us full of joy
One for every girl and boy
Lucky Moonstone — just for me"

Asa smiled at Humphrey. "Excellent. That
is what the young ones sang, in days of old.
I barely remember my moonstone. It was so
exciting for all the town to be alive with the
hunt. *Candy and Zurdy!* Everyone would get
involved in the fun.

Oola spoke up. "If everything was so
wonderful, how did the moonstones disappear?
Where are they?"

Asa answered her. "When I was very young..."

Chapter 12
The Legend of the Moonstones

It was the first Spring day in Mayfield. Dozens of trolls were frolicking and dancing in the streets and lawns. Trolls were dancing on the tops of the thatched huts and running through town with hoops and balls.

In the center of town, twelve trolls were playing around a giant Maypole with streaming laced strands hanging from the top of the pole. Each troll, in various colors of dress and hair, danced about the pole, trying to play the game. The colors of the strands matched the colors of the individual trolls' hair, so that they could tell who the winner was.

Suddenly, the sound of a horn was heard, far

away. As the horn came closer, one could hear a lovely, compelling, simple fanfare. As each troll heard the sound, they smiled, stopped their activity, and arranged themselves along the streets. The feeling of anticipation was delicious as the trolls chattered and murmured.

At the far end of town, shouts of, "Here they are!" were heard, and the parade began. Trolls in fancy dress uniform, shiny gold accents, banners, batons, flags, and streamers paraded into town, cheered on by the crowd. Lastly, the Mayor of Mayfield, Lord Hoodoo, entered on his wheeled cart, pulled by muscular trolls. Everyone cheered and he waved back in a dignified fashion, nodding to some, acknowledging others with clasped hands, or a slight wave of a curved hand held only head-high. Nothing too exuberant for Lord Hoodoo.

Behind Lord Hoodoo were the troll children, none of whom had a moonstone. They knew that this was the day to find their moonstones. Some of them seemed young, maybe too young, and anxious. Indeed a few of them were even a little whiny about being there, and were walking alongside their mothers, clinging and hiding. Others were oblivious to the day, just enjoying marching in the parade.

The parade came to a halt in the center of the town square, and the crowd continued to chatter happily until Lord Hoodoo stepped up to the speaker's podium. He raised his hand solemnly.

"Citizens of Mayfield, greetings!" shouted Lord Hoodoo.

Trolls responded with a hearty "Greetings" back at his Lordship, except for one loudmouth who yelled, "Hiya, Hoodoo!" This won a little chuckle out of a few trolls, and a brief look of admonishment from His Lordship. He recovered his composure quickly.

"Happy Spring Day to all, and congratulations to our twelve baby trolls who will seek their moonstones today!"

The crowd responded with a hurrah.

"You know the rules: one stone to a troll, no fighting, and no magic until you meet with your moonstone counselor."

The crowd responded with, "Yah, right."

Lord Hoodoo looked around, paused, and then, with a broad grin on his face, said, "Well, what are you waiting for? The stones won't find themselves."

The crowd cheered, and most of the children dispersed tugging on their parents. The few whiny ones were led by their mothers, and a few seemed to prefer picking flowers, but most scampered off in all directions, wide-eyed and happy.

One troll stood alone, blinking, looking quite lost. He was Hubert, and no one seemed to even notice him. After a few moments, he started to shuffle off in one direction, turned, looked around, tried another direction, and then stopped again.

Newberry, one of the Mayor's entourage, noticed Hubert, and gasped. He ran up to Candy, a fellow committee member, and spoke in whispers with great agitation. "Candy, what about Hubert? Has someone taken over for his poor dear father?"

Candy became greatly concerned, "No one is helping him? I thought after his father died someone would help out."

"We talked about this in committee. Oh, you weren't there that day. Well, someone was supposed to volunteer."

Candy looked at Newberry. "Well, you'd better go see about him."

Newberry was taken aback. "You know I can't do that. I am in charge of the food service. It's the most complicated event of the year, and Mayor Hoodoo is counting on me."

Candy looked at Hubert. "I mean, look at him. He's all alone out there; I'm sure he's completely lost. It's so sad." Then Candy looked at Newberry. "I'll take over for you until you get back with Hubert." Candy started pushing Newberry towards the young troll.

Newberry only slightly resisted. "Candy, the banquet is my job, and my whole reputation. If it is not done right, it will be my future going down the drain."

Candy said, "And who taught you to make Razzleberry dressing just the way Hoodoo likes it? Me, that's who. Now, trust me to do this, and go be Hubert's father for the Moonstone

Quest." With that, Candy turned back and joined the trolls unloading the food racks from the carts.

Newberry took a last look at Candy handling the banquet preparations and shrugged. Then he turned and saw Hubert sitting in the dust in the middle of the square, staring off into nothing. Newberry choked back a sob and composed himself. He approached Hubert and squatted next to him.

"Hello, Hubert."

Hubert looked up, and replied in a dry voice, "Hi, Uncle Newbie."

Newberry continued. "Let's you and I go find that special moonstone, shall we?"

Hubert looked at his feet. "It's okay, you don't have to come. I'll go find it."

Newberry looked around to see if anyone was watching, and then sat in the dust next to Hubert, facing him. "Your father and I were good friends, you know that, don't you?"

Hubert nodded and looked at his feet.

Newberry continued. "I told him more than once that if there was something I could do to help you two, I would be glad to."

Hubert was unmoved.

Newberry continued. "You know how sometimes, if you can help somebody, you feel good? You know how, when you do something that nobody else can do, and you do it, you feel glad? "

Hubert thought for a minute. "I guess."

Newberry continued. "Well, I like to help people—it makes me feel so special and useful. And sometimes, I need people to help me out, you know?"

Hubert did not reply.

Newberry continued. "So, Hubert, you can help me today. I made a promise to your father, and you can help me keep it. The way to keep my promise is for the two of us, you and me, to go together to find that moonstone."

Hubert looked up at Newberry. "So, I would be helping you?"

Newberry smiled. "Yep. You are the only person in the whole forest who can help me today. I really need you."

Hubert smiled back. "Okay, Uncle Newbie."

The two trolls stood and began dusting off. Hubert asked, "So, which way do we go?"

Newberry replied, "Your Moonstone is calling you. You have to listen with your ears, your senses, your spirit."

Hubert closed his eyes and listened, then opened them. "I don't hear it. What does it sound like?"

Newberry was momentarily confused, then recovered. "Oh, it's...uh...it's like...um..." Newberry pulled out his own moonstone and held it out for Hubert to touch but didn't let go of it. "Here, see if mine speaks to you."

Hubert reached out to touch Newberry's stone. When he touched it, his eyes opened wide, "Cool!" Hubert looked around quickly and rushed off into the forest. "Come on!"

It was late afternoon. Hubert was walking around a raised mound of dirt, grass, and hard scrub. Newberry was staggering behind him, and finally plopped down on a fallen tree. "Hubert, wait. I think we've reached a dead end. You've walked around this place twice already. Just give it up until tomorrow."

Hubert was searching the mound of grass even harder. "We can't. It's here. I can hear it loud and clear."

Newberry looked at the sun low in the sky. "We have to get back for the banquet. We don't want to miss that. There's guzzlenut tarts and angel cake. Now, that's enough looking for today. It's almost sunset."

Hubert was pulling at some vines and trying to clear away branches from the knoll. "I want my moonstone. It's here, in here." Suddenly Hubert gave a little shriek. "A cave! There's something in this cave!"

Newberry looked very concerned, and rushed to Hubert's side, trying to look where Hubert was looking. "Be careful! Do you see any bears or anything? I don't want to have to explain everything to a bear. They are really slow on the uptake sometimes."

Hubert looked anxiously at Newberry. "Can you get some light? Can you see in there? My moonstone is calling to me, but there's no light."

Newberry began to protest but decided it

would be quickest to just show Hubert that there was nothing there. He called out softly, "Shiners! Lightning bugs! Beamers! Come quickly now. I need you to show us this cave." Suddenly, dozens, then a hundred shining lightning bugs gathered at the mouth of the cave and entered where Newberry showed them. "That's right, thank you. A few more, please."

Newberry bent down and entered the small mouth of the cave, where Hubert had already scampered through. Inside, the bugs lit the way, but it was a small cave. Newberry shook his head wearily and said. "Okay, Hubert, there's nothing..."

"Here! In this pool of water. Look, Uncle Newbie. Bring the lights here."

Newberry urged the bugs forward and peered into the pool over Hubert's shoulder. He almost stumbled over what he saw.

There were dozens of stones just below the surface of the little pool of water. They were glowing, swirling mixtures in every color, and almost uniform in shape and size.

Hubert bent down with both hands outstretched, and Newberry stopped him. "Wait a minute. Which one is yours?"

Hubert tried to shake off Newberry. "All of them. I found them."

Newberry stopped Hubert again. "No, not all of them, Hubert. Only one of them is yours. You heard it calling to you. Which one is it?"

Hubert said, "Let me go. They are all mine."

Newberry was losing his struggle with Hubert now. "Just one, that's all a troll gets. You can't have more than one moonstone."

Hubert shook free of Newberry and plunged his hands into the pool. His hands brought up dirt and rocks and pebbles, but no moonstones. "Where did they go?" He splashed and reached again and again but came up empty each time.

Chapter 13
The Greedy Troll

Oola and Humphrey were as quiet as Jerry and me until this point, and then they started sobbing like babies, holding each other, their hair mussed up with their tears. They must have had no idea about this Hubert troll.

I wanted to cry, too. But Jerry said, "So all the moonstones turned to rocks?"

"The moonstone was there, in the water, for Hubert to pick his own," said Asa.

"It really was? It wasn't just a trick of the lightning bugs' lights?" said Humphrey.

"Are you saying Hubert got what he deserved?" said Oola.

Asa paused before answering. "No one

deserves to be left out, abandoned, or cheated. But when these things happen, and they will occasionally happen, how we react is what is important."

"Poor Hubert," I said.

"Yeah, no father," said Oola.

"Just this weird Uncle Newbie; what's up with that?" said Jerry.

"And then no moonstone," said Humphrey.

"So now you'll tell us what happened to Hubert," said Humphrey.

"He got mad and burned the town down," laughed Jerry.

I was furious. "Stop that!"

Asa said, "Oh, no. That is not what happened. What happened was much worse! " And she continued telling us the tale while the campfire burned low.

* * *

The feeling burned inside Hubert. Everyone else had a father and mother. Everyone else had a family. Everyone else had a moonstone. But not him. What kind of world would that be? What kind of troll didn't have a magic moonstone? Everyone else had everything they wanted. Hubert would get even.

The story of the moonstone that turned to rocks came out. Other trolls tried to be nice, but he hated it. It was like pity. He knew they were making fun of him, laughing behind his back. He would show them.

He thought about it for seven years. He saw seven more groups of trolls—babies all of them—go through the moonstone quest and find their moonstones. He listened, hopefully at first, for any stone calling out to him. None ever did. Eventually he just quit listening, because it only got his hopes up. He knew, more clearly than ever, what he was going to do.

It seemed like a really difficult thing, but in the end, it was so easy. He planned to go around the village with a sack, like Santa Claus, but instead of bringing presents, he would pick up moonstones. And he couldn't just take one or two, or a few. Trolls would know.

He would have to take them all. That was the hard part. Leave no stone unturned. He actually

laughed out loud at his little joke. He decided
this would be the night, and he was ready.

The first hut was Candy's. Candy was
sleeping on her cot, moonstone held in her
two hands. Hubert looked at her with mixed
feelings in his heart. On the one hand, she was
the one troll who was nice to Hubert no matter
what. She would give him a smile when she
saw him, and it was a genuine smile that said
she was happy to see him. Even when he was
grumpy and unkind, she would laugh it off and

still be gracious. He picked her cottage to start with on purpose. He thought if he could start there, then every other troll would be easier.

He wondered how in the world he was going to take this stone from her two hands. He thought about tickling her arm so she would move it or drop the stone. In the end, he just reached over and removed the moonstone from Candy's hands. She stirred uneasily but did not awaken. Even in the dim light Hubert could see the smile fade from her face.

After that first one, he got busy. The little town was small, but still he had to visit each and every cottage. What if someone were awake early, or had trouble falling asleep? He would proceed with caution, but he would keep going.

And in the end, he picked up every single moonstone in Mayfield.

Hubert seemed to feel more powerful. He knew his power did not come from the moonstones. They would not work for him. His power did not come from the theft. He realized his feeling of power came from the fear that the trolls would have when they realized what had happened. They would not be angry at him, they would fear him. This was a delicious feeling for him.

He could simply hide the moonstones, but there would be no one to guard them. He could throw them over the great waterfall, but that would not be any better. The trolls would keep searching. He had thought about this for years and had a much better plan.

He had created a riddle, as the wise ones of ancient days had done, and only by solving the riddle could the trolls find the moonstones.

But even then, the moonstones were tucked away in a strong chest of oak and iron, with reinforced bands all the way around it. Hubert put the chest on the back of the giant turtle that lives in the Great Lake beyond the edge of the forest. He floated in a boat and the turtle swam alongside, as they traveled to the island in the center of the lake. There, he knew of hidden caves, a maze of caverns where he could hide the chest.

Finally, for those who solved the puzzle, reached the island, ventured through the caves,

and found the chest, a new surprise awaited
them. The lock he devised would show them all
how he felt.

* * *

Jerry spoke up. "Well, if you know where the
thing is, why don't you go and get it?"

Asa seemed to be thinking this over.

"You must hear more of the story before you
understand."

* * *

Something very important happened when
Hubert got the chest into the cave in its hiding
place. Hubert heard his moonstone.

He was sure. He heard his own moonstone
sounding out to him, even inside the recesses
of the cave. He left the cave, returned, by
great hardship, through the lake and back to
Mayfield, to the place where his moonstone
was singing to him. He approached the stream,
looked down, and saw his stone, clear and blue,
shinier than the rest. He bent down, picked it
up out of the water, and held it.

His joy seemed endless. Shivers of relief and thanksgiving coursed throughout his whole body. He wanted to cry out loud. He wanted to show everyone. Then he remembered what he had done. And a great chasm formed in his mind. A part of him was saddened, sickened, appalled at his deed, and he wished to return the moonstones to every troll. The other part of him was vengeful, glad to have his when no one else had theirs, thinking he finally got what he deserved.

Someone was standing next to him. It was Candy. The sun was just breaking over the horizon and the trees were scattering the light around them. Still Hubert's moonstone shone brightly. Hubert looked from his moonstone to Candy, and then faced her.

"What do you want?"

"Oh, Hubert. It looks like you finally found your moonstone! That's wonderful. We must tell the others."

"No, don't tell anyone. But where is your stone?"

Candy looked very sad and confused. "Well,

I really don't know. I had it last night, but this morning, well, it's gone. I'm looking for it now, but I don't think it is here."

"I know where." Hubert said this before he even meant to. But once he said it, it was done.

Candy gasped. "You know where my moonstone is?"

Hubert set his face hard and looked away, to the sky, the trees, anywhere but at Candy's face. "I stole it. I stole them all. They are mine, and I have hidden them. Beyond the lake. Beneath the sleeping volcano. Inside the deepest cave. With a magical spell that no troll will be able to undo."

Candy stepped backwards, away from Hubert, but he stopped her with a look. He told her the great riddle, and when he was sure she had heard every word, he turned and left.

Hubert had his moment when he could have taken the right path. But he refused. And once he made up his mind, he began to sink deeper into darkness. He realized he could not even keep his own moonstone, for fear that someone would take it from him. So back he went, across the Great Lake, to the island, into the caverns, to the chest of stones, where he hid the very last one.

* * *

All of us were holding our breath as Asa finished the story. "We don't know where Hubert hid the stones. Some of this is just legend or mystery. But I wanted to tell you all I know of the story."

Jerry, for once completely into the story, asked, "So where is Hubert? What happened to him?"

Asa said, "We are not sure. These things happened a long time ago. No one has ever seen him again."

Asa looked at Oola and Humphrey. "Humphrey, do you know why we have the sports games each year in the fall?"

"To choose the strongest troll!"

Asa said, "Yes, but why do we do this?"

Humphrey looked puzzled. "Umm, he gets a trophy!"

We laughed at that. The laughter seemed

extra-loud, because we had all this tension built up inside us.

Oola said, "Does it have something to do with Hubert and the story of the moonstones?"

Asa continued. "We have competitions for superior senses, and we give awards for trolls who show gifted abilities for intelligence. And don't we also honor trolls who serve others, giving of their time to help needy trolls?"

Oola said, "Yes. And Humphrey wins awards all the time for his excellent hearing, eyesight, smell, and his sense of direction."

Humphrey blushed deeply at this unexpected compliment. "Oh, gee, Oolie, lots of trolls can see as well as me."

Asa said, "But none better, Humphrey. You are gifted in many ways, my young friend."

Then Asa looked at us all. "Four awards for four trolls. These games and competitions have been held for many years. But they started in these dark times, after the moonstones were taken away."

Humphrey said, "I'm really lost, Asa. What does one have to do with the other?"

Asa seemed much sadder then. "Hubert could not just hide the moonstones, as you know. And he could not just do away with them – they would never disappear or be destroyed. He had to make them unreachable. After years of watching the other trolls, he devised a riddle. All the older trolls know it. You young ones may have heard one of us mention parts of it, but no one speaks of it anymore except in hushed tones, and only portions."

Oola said, "What is the riddle? Can you tell us?"

> *Look with your eyes*
> *Think with your mind*
> *Strive with your hands*
> *Your heart should be kind*
> *But even if you reach the end*
> *The one who is not one will win*

All of us were quiet. I could see each face in the firelight twisting and pondering, trying to figure out the answer to the riddle. I mean, it was so short. Each phrase was simple enough.

"*Look with your eyes.*" I knew how to do that. "*Think with your mind.*" Okay, that's always a good plan. "*Strive with your hands.*" Sounds like something we can all do. "*Your heart should be kind.*" Glad to know about that.

But the last part. What is that all about? "Even if you reach the end / The one who is not one…"

Oola finally said what we were all thinking. "Asa, have you solved the riddle? What does it mean?"

Asa sounded much less sure of herself for the first time. "My child, no troll really knows. What we have done, for these long many years, is to try and find a troll who lives up to these expectations. Superior in eyesight and the senses, wise in intellect, strong in body, and full of kindness. The four trophies. No one troll has met these qualifications."

Oola thought about that a while. "But maybe, it's not supposed to be in just one troll. Maybe a partnership."

Asa stood up. "Two trolls, and two…humans. Your new friends."

Jerry spoke up. "Hey, neat. We're like the solution to the riddle."

I had to ask something. "But, Asa, what about the last part? What does it mean, *the one who is not one*'?"

"I do not yet know, but I feel the answer is close."

I just kept thinking about it. "Umm, the one what?"

Oola said, without even looking at me, "The one troll, I guess."

Then, like in slow motion, Oola, Humphrey, Asa all turned and looked at me. Not exactly at me, but at my hands. There I was, holding Binky, not even thinking about it. Everyone was looking at Binky.

Chapter 14
Decision

Jerry spoke up. "Winnie, put your doll away. No one here wants to see the doll when we have real live trolls to talk to."

I said, "Jerry, haven't you been listening? This doll, this Binky, this troll is the *'one who is not one.'* The last part of the riddle."

Oola and Humphrey looked at Asa, who nodded. "The four who take the journey must be friends, dedicated to the cause, determined to finish the task they begin. Of those I see in front of me, I see one who is keen of senses, one who is intelligent above the others, one who is kind and loving, and...," Asa looked at Jerry. "One who is stronger than any troll."

"Me?" said Jerry.

Asa continued. "The four of you can do this. In fact, I think you were destined to meet this way and save the trolls from extinction."

All around the campfire gasped. I said, "Extinction?"

Oola and Humphrey held on to each other. Oola said, "Oh no!"

Asa continued. "The moonstones are not merely adornments or tools. They are part of our life, our community. Without them, the trolls' life energy fades."

Humphrey cried out, "I'm feeling faint already!"

Oola rebuked him. "It's not happening that fast, Hump." Then she looked at Asa. "Is it?"

Asa said, "Trolls were meant to be happy and young, but more of us are aging and weak. Unless the stones are returned, we will continue to age.

Oola said, "Like your mother, Aerona?"

Asa said, "Yes. She is dying. And when she dies, she will be the first for us all."

I said, "But, why can't you all go together, the whole town? Go across the Great Lake and to the mountain to retrieve the stones? Maybe if you all try…"

Asa smiled. "My precious child, if only it were that easy. Years ago, trolls did try. No one was able to find the mountain or make even part of the journey successfully. Hubert put every kind of hindrance in our path. Now, after all these years, the legend seems more myth."

Humphrey said, "So, we might succeed because…I'm not getting it. What's different?"

Asa said, "You are different. You are the answer to the riddle. You are the strong body…"

At this, Jerry sat up quite straight.

"…keen senses…"

Humphrey smiled broadly.

"…superior mind…"

Oola blushed a purple shade obvious even in the firelight.

"…and a heart that is pure."

I wondered if she meant me. I didn't feel so pure.

Jerry said, "Hey, I've got a pure heart, too."

Asa stood up, and the trolls did also. "Follow your heart. Use your mind. Feel the way. Be strong. Each of you must help, or all will fail."

I said, "We will."

Jerry shook his head. "Wait a minute. You are thinking that these two trolls, and Winnie and I are going to find the moonstones that have been lost, hidden for years?"

I got up and grabbed my backpack. "Yes, we are. You're coming along."

Jerry stammered, "We can't just leave Dad."

"Leave him a note. We'll be back."

Oola, Humphrey, and I began marching along the path into the forest.

Jerry grabbed a scrap of paper and a pencil, scribbled a quick note, and left it on the windshield of the SUV. Then he took off to catch up. He screeched to a stop, returned for his backpack, and headed off again.

Asa remained behind. When I glanced back, did I see a faint smile on her lips?

Chapter 15
Journey

It's a good thing I didn't know what was going to happen that night as we began the walk. If I had known...

Anyway, there we were, walking along the forest trail. They were moving pretty fast for six-inch trolls. But Jerry and I had legs that were longer than six inches. We were inching along, and it was just ridiculous.

Jerry said, "This will take 'til Christmas, guys."

I said, "This is going awfully slow, Oola."

"Well, how about if I ride on your backpack? I'm not afraid now."

It seemed like a perfect idea, so I said, "Sure, come on up! Jerry, you let Humphrey ride on your pack."

Jerry stopped and had this weird, frozen, half-smile on his face. He stammered, "Uh, the troll is going to, like, hitch a ride...on my backpack...with me?"

I bent down and Oola scampered quickly up my backpack and stood on the fabric. She was just the right height to see over my shoulder as she stood behind me.

"Look, Jerry, it's cool. Just let the Humpster ride with you."

Humphrey giggled. "Humpster! That's so funny!"

Jerry made a forced smile, then he started to bend down lower to the ground. "Ok, Humphrey Humpster. I guess you can come up."

Humphrey was just about as scared as Jerry, from what I could tell. But Oola was encouraging him, so he climbed up Jerry's pack.

Humphrey's footsteps tickled Jerry. "Oh, gee, hey, what?" Jerry was wriggling around, and poor Humphrey almost fell off three times, but finally got to the top of the pack, and held on.

"Hey, you're a lot heavier than you look," Jerry added as we started walking again.

Poor Humphrey suddenly frowned and pouted, but Oola saved the day. She said, "Hump, Jerry means that you weigh more than that doll we found. . ."

I said, "Binky."

Oola looked at me and smiled. "Binky, yes. Hump is a super-duper troll of strength and bravery. His head weighs more than that Binky doll of yours."

Humphrey suddenly looked sad again. "Now, why did you have to talk about how much my head weighs, Oolie? My head doesn't weigh that much. It's just right."

Oola quickly cut in. "That's right, Hump."

Humphrey kept going, though. "And my ears are just right, too."

Oola sighed. "There's nothing wrong with your ears, Hump."

Humphrey seemed to need a lot of reassurance tonight. "And my eyes are very powerful – I see much clearer and farther than most other trolls."

Oola looked at me and rolled her eyes, but said to Humphrey, "I have always said that your eyes are THE best in Mayfield…Uh, wait a minute, Winnie."

I was walking along the trail at a pretty good clip, because it was so easy to see the clear trail in the moonlight. I suddenly realized I had walked way past where we had been with Dad. I didn't know where I was.

Jerry realized it too. We both stopped walking. Jerry said, "So how do you know this is the way?"

Humphrey said, "We must follow the stream."

Oola broke in, "To the West."

Humphrey continued, "The birds say the stream leads to a lake."

Suddenly, this little stroll in the night forest seemed like an endless journey. I was so fired up and sure of myself just a few minutes ago, but now, I was scared. I mean, sheesh, we were depending on a couple of six-inch creatures to lead us through the forest in the middle of the night.

Humphrey was undaunted. He spoke a

little rhyme.

> *The stars guide at night*
> *The sun during the day*
> *The wind is to the west*
> *And the rivers flow that way.*

The way he said it was so simple and easy, I felt like I had heard it before, even though I know I hadn't. I asked Humphrey where he learned that.

Humphrey said, quite as a matter of fact, "That's a rhyme we learn in school. Trolls always know which way to go."

That made me feel better as we walked along. I hoped I would remember the way home later.

Chapter 16
Missing

As fast as Winnie's dad fell asleep the night before, he woke with the earliest light. He came out of his tent, still wearing his gaudy pajamas. He looked around, wearing a puzzled look. He put the logs on the fire and got the coffee ready and placed the pot of water to boil. Finally, he decided to risk a quiet call.

"Winnie! Jerry!" He didn't actually yell out, thinking there just might be other campers around. And besides, it was still quite early; it was an effort just to talk in whispers with the beautiful scenery of the forest surrounding him. But the quiet didn't seem right. Where were they? He decided he had better try harder.

"WINNIE! JERRY! You had better get

yourselves back here to this campsite by the time I count to three! I mean it! One…Two… Three!"

Then he looked at the SUV and noticed the paper on the windshield. He picked it up and read it. It was written in Jerry's careless scrawl.

Dad, we've gone on a long hike. Wait for us.

His eyes began to widen as the importance of the note sunk in. "I'm not believing this!" Then he started shouting. "Winnie! Jerry! Come back!"

He climbed to the top of the SUV cab and shouted from the top. "Jerry! Winnie! Where are you? Answer me!"

It was at that moment that he sprang into action. Unfortunately, he was precariously balanced on the top of the SUV cab, straddling the search lights. He lost his balance and toppled to the ground.

"Oooh" he groaned.

He then got up and limped to the tent. Quicker than one would expect, he emerged from the tent in full uniform as Captain James Carver, Dallas Police Force, Department of Investigation.

James walked briskly over to the SUV, read the note again, carefully folded it, tucked it into his uniform pocket. He reached inside the SUV and pulled out the CB Radio microphone. He switched on the radio and pressed the button to speak.

"This is Captain J. M. Carver, of the Dallas Investigation Unit, calling any Ranger Station Base within earshot of my call. Come in Base. Over."

There was a moment of static on the radio. Then, the speaker crackled a reply. The voice speaking had a decidedly country accent.

"This is Ranger Bob Wilson at the Pine Forest Station."

James spoke again. "We copy, Ranger Bob. We have a four-one-seven situation at campsite one-one-five. I am requesting assistance."

Ranger Bob replied patiently. Something about his reply might make the listener think that Ranger Bob was not convinced that this was a legitimate distress call. "Well, we're not used to those big city codes, Captain. Would you mind telling me what a four-one-seven is?"

James seemed a bit sheepish as he replied. "Oh, right. It's …uh …missing juvenile. In this case, it is my children. Winnie and Jerry. They are missing. Over."

Ranger Bob's voice suddenly took on a serious and alert tone. "I understand, Captain. I am prepared to offer any and all assistance. Over."

James seemed relieved. "We copy, Ranger Bob. My children left a note, so I plan to begin my search from this campsite, which is located ..." At this pause, James let go of the radio button while he looked for a map in the SUV.

The Ranger came back on the radio. "Breaking in, Carver. Did you say your children left a note, Over?"

James said, "That's right. The note says they went on a hike. Over."

The Ranger said, "When did you find that they were missing, Over?"

James said, "About five minutes ago. Over."

Ranger Bob's voice now became a bit impatient, and he seemed to be unhappy with the situation. "Captain Carver, maybe in Dallas you people live in the fast lane, but out here, children gone for five minutes are not 'missing'. Especially not when they left a note saying that they have gone hiking. Over."

James voice seemed to be losing his normally calm controlled tone. "But you don't know my kids! They would never go hiking together. They don't go anywhere together. They don't even like each other."

Suddenly James realized what he probably

sounded like to the Ranger. "I was exaggerating. They are good kids. I just..."

Ranger Bob seemed to ignore the remarks. "Look, this kind of thing happens all the time in the Park. Now, if your kids are still missing at nightfall, contact us again, and we'll come looking. Over."

James was furious. "Nightfall! My kids could be dead by then! I'll just look for them myself. Over and Out."

"Pine Forest base station clear."

James put down the CB radio, picked up the map of the Pine Forest, and began talking to himself in the clear calm voice of a police officer in charge of the situation.

"Let's see. I can start at the hiking trail head."

James put the map down and started the car. He raced the engine, checked the lights, put it in 4-wheel drive, and took off, spinning the wheels, unknowingly throwing dirt on the tent and messing up the camp as he went.

Chapter 17
Finding the Way

I woke up, and at first, I didn't know where I was. I saw Jerry sleeping a few feet away from me on the grass, and thought, "Where's Dad?" Then, Jerry moved and was about to smush Humphrey, so I yelled, and everyone woke up.

We had been walking for hours, so we found a spot to rest and made camp. It was the first time I had slept out in the open, really open, no house or tent or anything. I was a little stiff but felt pretty good. The warm sun was welcome after the nighttime start.

Jerry asked, yawning, "How much farther is it, anyway?"

Oola said, "Our journey has just started. I feel

it is still a long way."

Oola and Humphrey climbed onto our packs, and we resumed our journey downstream.

Humphrey recited:

> *The soft rain that falls*
> *The gentle breezes blow*
> *The sun up above*
> *Make the green grasses grow*

Jerry rolled his eyes and said, half-jokingly, "Are we going to hear poetry the whole way? 'Cause if we are, I'm just going to head back to camp."

I said, "I like it. It's nice. Like a song."

Humphrey was encouraged by that and said, "I know more."

> *The spirit of life*
> *Is present around us*
> *The maker of morning*
> *And beauty surrounds us*

* * *

In another part of the forest, James slowed the SUV to a stop at the road's end. He picked up the map and resumed speaking to himself.

"Let's see. They weren't on any of the forest roads, so that means they are either taking one of the hiking trails or are making their own way. Unless they're hurt."

James winced at his own idea and chided himself.

"Got to stop thinking that. They're fine. They're missing. They're out in the thousand-acre forest in October with no one else around for miles, but they're fine. At least I hope so. This would be a lot simpler in Dallas." James grabbed the shifter and put the SUV into gear. "Okay. Hiking trails, here we go."

James then went off-road with his 4x4 SUV, throwing dust and debris as he cut into hiking paths. A sign clearly showed a warning:

NO VEHICLES

* * *

After following the stream for a long while, with the tall trees and the forest growth, we almost stumbled into the lake. The edge of the forest came so quickly, and there was a tiny strip of sand and then this huge lake. There were a few cabins with piers leading into the lake, and to our left was a group of boats for rent, secured by ropes.

Jerry exclaimed, "Wow, look!"

I said, "It's so big! It looks like the ocean."

Jerry agreed, "Yeah, but no waves."

Oola said, "Humphrey, can you see the mountain?"

Humphrey was already straining his eyes looking out over the water. "It's…it's not there. I don't see it. Maybe this is the wrong lake."

Oola said, "It's the Great Lake."

Jerry scoffed. "It can't be the Great Lake. That's in Michigan, miles away."

I asked, "So, umm, do you call this giant turtle or something? I've been thinking maybe we don't need the turtle if we could find a boat."

Humphrey said, "I'm afraid we don't know any turtles." He paused and said, "Not very well, anyway. We're just on speaking terms. Barely."

I said, "Come on." We all went over to the boat rental place, but it was deserted, like everything else.

Jerry said, "One of these canoes would be great, but they are all tied and locked."

I noticed two more on the side of the building. "What about these? They're not tied up."

Jerry said, "Sure, but we can't rent them."

"We could borrow one. There are even two life jackets here."

"Borrow? As in, take without permission? Not sure that's borrowing."

"Come on, Jerry. We'll return it when we come back."

"Well, I guess."

I said, "So let's get going."

Jerry said, "Wait, umm, what if they are over here because something's wrong with them?"

I said, "Then we won't use that one. Now come on."

Jerry walked over to the green boat and began lifting one end. I stopped him.

"Let's take the yellow one."

Jerry began to get even more exasperated. "What difference does it make whether we drown in the green one or the yellow one or the polka-dotted one?"

Humphrey said, "I don't see a polka-dotted boat. Are my eyes going bad? Am I color blind?"

Oola ignored Humphrey. "Jerry, the yellow one will be easier to see from far away."

Jerry picked up one side of the yellow boat, dragged it to the water's edge, threw in two paddles, and said, "I feel like a pirate." We donned our life jackets.

Once we figured out which way to point the canoe, and how to team paddle, we steered the plastic yellow canoe into the middle of the Great Lake, with Humphrey and Oola on our backs.

Jerry said, "So, don't forget. We promise to return this thing when we get back."

I said, "To the very spot we picked it up."

Chapter 18
Searching

James halted the SUV at the edge of a cliff. He consulted the map again and spoke his thoughts aloud.

"That takes care of the hiking trails. What next? Where would I go if I were a 11-year-old girl with her 12-year-old brother?"

He paused for a moment.

"To the mall. But we don't have a mall in the forest."

He flipped the map upside down and right side up again.

"Oh, this map is useless. This search is useless."

James looked out into the forest and thought. "Maybe they're exploring that cave we found.

They might not be so afraid of the bats now."

He put the SUV into gear, backed up, and roared off looking for the cave, which was actually in the cliff just below him.

* * *

We had been paddling and resting for, it seemed like, an hour. We'd look back at the shore and the tree line, and then we'd keep trying to steer straight. Jerry had a pocket compass; I saw him check it a couple of times. And Humphrey would get kind of spacey-eyed and peer out from Jerry's shoulder and point like some kind of sailor man and say, "More this way." So, Jerry and I would shift our paddles and do what he said.

It had been sunny and almost too hot to be doing this, but the sun went behind some clouds, and then it got overcast. Without talking, both Jerry and I stopped paddling, and the boat drifted along in the same direction.

Jerry turned to Humphrey. "Okay, Hump. Which way?"

Humphrey blinked at Jerry. "Which way?"

Jerry said, "Yeah, time to use those eyes and ears, the best directional finders in the universe..."

I said, "Jerry, don't hurt his feelings."

And Jerry kept on, "...or at least in the forest. Tell us which way to point."

Humphrey said quietly, "Which way?"

I said, "Oola, every way seems the same. "

Oola said, in the same weird quiet voice, "The same?"

I was getting exasperated with all this hemming and hawing. "So, which way should we go?"

Now, Oola started getting creepy. "Go?"

Jerry blew out a huge breath. "Well, the boat seems to know which way to go. It's doing just fine without us even rowing."

The boat was moving along on its own just like it had a silent motor or something. There was even a wake behind us. Things were feeling very strange.

Jerry was getting out his compass again, "So is it North, South, East, or West? Which way do we steer?"

Humphrey was looking as green as his hair. "Steer?"

"Yeah, steer, as in aim." Jerry looked down at his compass and then did a double take. "Hey, what's the deal? The needle's going crazy! I can't tell which way is North. What in the world would cause the needle to spin around like that?"

I was listening to Jerry, but barely. The boat was going really fast now, without anyone paddling it. Oola and Humphrey started moaning, which was totally creepy. I looked out

at the water.

"Oh my gosh! Look!"

Just ahead of us the whole lake was swirling down a giant drain, and we were in this tiny canoe, being sucked in.

Jerry screamed, "WHIRLPOOL!"

There was nothing we could do! We screamed and grabbed onto each other for dear life! Then the boat started to spin like we were going down the drain. We were being pulled under, all of us still screaming!

We dropped through the middle of the whirlpool and splashed onto another lake. We hit so hard I don't know how we didn't topple over. The sky was completely overcast, fog and the mist were everywhere, and we couldn't see a shore, or a water line, or anything. All we could see was fog.

Humphrey was moaning the loudest and just kept saying, "Ooh, I'm dizzy."

Oola said, "I have a headache."

Jerry said, "Where are we?"

"I can't see." What I meant was, I couldn't see anything beyond the boat, but it didn't matter.

No one cared what I said.

"I'm dizzy," Humphrey repeated.

Oola said, "I have a MAJOR headache."

Jerry said, "This place is weird. Are we, like, in the same lake as before?"

Humphrey moaned, and recited his little poem, but sadly, with different words.

No sun at day
No stars at night
No wind to feel
No waters bright

I almost cried, but what good would it have done? So I said, "What are we going to do?"

"We can't go back," Jerry said. "it's like a toilet bowl or something."

Humphrey finally seemed to come to his senses, "Then we go forward."

Oola said, "Just – talk softly, okay?"

Jerry and I picked up the paddles and started rowing.

Chapter 19
That Sinking Feeling

James Carver had taken his SUV into places it had never been, and wasn't intended to go. It seemed to shudder with fear each time it dipped and bumped along the forest floor. It was the off-road vehicle that had never been off-road. It was the 4x4 from an urban setting, now lost in the Pine Texas State Forest. It had been used to nice, steady concrete and asphalt roads, not the jolting and tossing that it was being put through now. Which is why things started coming loose, and connections started unconnecting, and the SUV began to lose heart.

After one particularly severe bump, the SUV instrument panel lit up, and the engine stopped. James looked at the panel and decided that his SUV just stalled. He grabbed the key and twisted it to restart the engine. Nothing happened. He tried the ignition again. There was a weak turning sound, but no starting. He looked again at the instrument panel, and saw a light that said, "Service Engine Fool".

James shook his head, did a double take, and looked again. It actually said "Soon" or maybe it was an error code. But his car was stopped, and he had a sinking feeling.

It was more than a sinking feeling. His tires were sinking. He looked around as the trees seem to get taller and the mud came up slowly to cover the doors.

"What is this? Mud? MUD!" He tried to open the doors, but they were sealed tightly. He quickly lowered the window and climbed out of it, getting caught in the seatbelt, and then uncaught. The only place for him to go was up, so he climbed onto the roof of the car, and watched it sink a few more inches. It seemed to stop, and it was obvious it was not going to move again.

But James was stuck, on top of the SUV, in

the middle of a huge mud puddle. Or was he?
He looked at the direction he came from. His
car had jumped quite a large log to get into this
quagmire. He had to try and get back to the log
and the forest. But if he jumped to the log, that
would certainly hurt, and maybe he'd fall back
into the swamp.

He looked up at the trees and saw a lot of
branches and growth. Although he had no

delusions that he was Tarzan, he decided to try a swing off the car roof and onto the land beyond the log.

He saw that there was only one branch he could try for. Gingerly, he stepped forward, and the car began tilting and sinking more. He stepped back quickly. He began talking aloud again.

"Okay, Carver. You have one chance and one chance only. Get to shore or fall into the swamp. Make it to safety or die in the woods. Save your children or…"

There was no alternative to that. He would save his children; that was everything. How could he go home and face his wife without… Now he really had to stop thinking like that. It was not his wife Helen that he feared. It was failing. James hated to fail. He could compromise, negotiate, or consent, but he could not fail. As a man. As a father. As a police officer. Failure was not an option.

With no further thought, with no detailed planning, with only a gigantic force of will and strength, he leaped forward from the back of the SUV, grabbed the branch, and held on. But the branch was not sturdy. It dropped him directly into the swampy mire behind the SUV.

He hit the mud almost in a sitting position, which was fortunate. It slowed his descent more than if he had plunged in feet first like a knife. But it hurt. He still had the broken branch in his hands. He pulled on more low growth, dragged himself to the log, and to safety.

As he stood up, covered in muck, and looked back at the sunken SUV which had his cell phone, CB radio, in fact, many of the things he needed just to get through a day in his job, he shouted, "NOOOOO!"

Chapter 20
The Mysterious Island

After paddling for what seemed like another hour, I was really tired. We still couldn't see any kind of shoreline or reference point through the fog and mist. The water had been really smooth, but we were suddenly bobbing up and down.

"What's causing all this wave action?"

Jerry shrugged, "I don't know. Maybe the wind is...."

Suddenly the boat hit something hard and we jolted forward. Humphrey held on to Jerry's backpack, and Oola to mine, and somehow, they didn't fall out. We had landed on a beach!

Oola scampered down from my pack, jumped up on the front of the canoe, and looked around. Humphrey joined her up there, they looked straight ahead, then slowly raised their heads together – two big bunches of troll hair tilting back in unison.

Oola said, "Humphrey..."

"I know."

Together, they said with awe, "Troll Mountain."

I didn't see anything special about this place. It was a really tiny beach, just a bit of sand, and growth all around. I looked up and saw this huge mountain. The more I looked, the more it resembled a volcano.

Jerry decided he had enough "Well, we made it. No moonstones. Ready to go back? Good. Let's start back."

I agreed with him and grabbed the paddles to row the other way. But it was no good. A large wave washed us up onto the shore, then went back out. We would have to climb out of the boat, lift it up, turn it around, and struggle against the waves.

Oola and Humphrey turned around to look at us. Boy, was I ashamed. We had come all this way, and I was too afraid to do anything.

Jerry said, "Well, we've come this far. Might as well see what's here."

"It's better than the whirlpool," I added.

So, we grabbed our packs and Oola and Humphrey took off into the jungle growth. Jerry and I followed, or at least tried to. A couple of times, they scooted off in some direction so deep in the undergrowth that we had to call out for them. As much as I didn't want to be here, I sure didn't want to be lost here.

I actually wished I was back in camp with Dad.

* * *

At that moment, Winnie's dad was falling into the fishing pond that they had enjoyed the previous day. He meant to just stop by the side and wash off some of the mud but lost his balance and splashed into the pond.

He felt foolish about falling, but it really was the quickest way to get all washed off. So, he made an impromptu bath and almost started enjoying himself. Then he stopped.

He felt something in the water, but what? It was probably a plant or tiny fish or something. It was nothing. He didn't have to worry about that.

Then he stopped again. He stood waist high in the water, very still. He listened. What *was* that? A kind of splash? No, maybe a swoosh? He looked behind him and saw a fish coming straight at him.

"Ol' Blue!" He yelled and struggled to get to the pier again. It was really hard moving fast in the water, at least, hard for a man. Not hard for a gigantic fish, swimming straight for him, with one purpose in mind.

He would not be able to make the pier in time – that fish was coming really fast – so he turned around and made loud splashing noises with his fist and his arms, yelling and slapping the water. He turned and struggled to the pier some more, and then stopped again and made the same splashy noises. He finally reached the broken pier and pulled himself up, just as Ol' Blue reached him and made a leap in the air. James thought the fish would actually snap at him, but the giant fish was apparently only showing off and fell back into the water, moving away once again.

James sat on the jagged edge of the pier but made sure no part of him hung off the edge. He shivered a bit in the cold and decided he would let the sun dry him off. He lay flat on the pier boards, and yelled out, "Winnie! Jerry! WHERE ARE YOU?"

Chapter 21
The Deep Dark Cave

I knew we were getting closer to the sleeping volcano, but it didn't seem like it. The growth was so thick, and we just had one thing to do; follow Oola and Humphrey.

Jerry spoke. "Well, this is fun. Hiking through thick forest on some long-lost island with no cell phone and no way to get help."

"Jerry," I said. "We have to help the trolls find their moonstones."

"This is hopeless. There are no moonstones here," he said as he swatted at bugs. "Only giant mosquitoes. Ouch."

Oola and Humphrey stopped directly in front of a cave opening. They were whispering to each other. Then I remembered something.

"Oola, didn't Asa tell us the trolls' moonstones were in a cave?"

Oola turned around to face me. "Yes." She said it weird, like she was anxious, scared, and excited all at once.

Jerry said, "Well, Hump. What do your ears say about this place? Any moonstones calling out?"

I was just about to hit him for the hundredth time, when he realized how he sounded. He got down on his knees and said, rather kindly, "I mean, is this the place?"

Humphrey seemed as scared and excited as Oola. They looked at one another.

I said, "What is it?"

Oola hesitated, and then blurted out, "The cave is dark."

Humphrey said, "Very dark."

Jerry looked at the cave entrance. "It's a pretty big cave, though. Even I can fit through the entrance. Don't be scared."

Oola bristled and her hair shot up at the comment. "Oola is not afraid of the dark."

Jerry said, "Well okay. If we need to go in

there, let's go."

Just as Jerry was about to go in, Oola added, "Oola is afraid of the creatures that live in the dark."

Jerry nearly fell as he scrambled backwards. "Creatures? What creatures?"

I must have sounded worried too. "Oh no, worse than bats?"

"Humphrey can hear...strange sounds. Voices."

Somehow, voices sounded much worse to me than creatures. "What are they saying?"

Humphrey said, "I don't know. I cannot make them out clearly, but they seem threatening. Oola hears them differently from me."

Oola said, "Hubert hid the moonstones, and if this is the cave..."

Humphrey said. "Could he still be alive? Or are the voices echoes from long ago?"

I said, "Can we just cover our ears or something?"

Oola and Humphrey once again whispered to each other, and then turned to look at us.

"Humphrey says we will all hear the voices as

we get farther in."

Humphrey said, "Just keep together, hold each other's hands, and don't listen to anyone but us."

Jerry said, "This is very confusing, Hump. Is anyone in there?"

Humphrey said, "Block out the voices, just keep going."

So, Jerry and I held hands, Oola held on to my pack, and Humphrey to Jerry's. We could only move slowly, which was fine by me. They made it sound so mysterious, but we started to go through the entrance.

It was really dark, I mean, pitch dark. I kept expecting my eyes to get used to the darkness and I would be able to make out the walls or the floor or something. There was only the faintest light behind me from the entrance. I could hear Jerry breathing, or maybe it was Oola in my ear.

Suddenly I felt guilty for being scared. And I felt guilty for leaving Dad at the campsite. And I felt bad about stealing the canoe, even though we planned to return it later.

I felt like I was just a bad person and had done nothing good ever in my life. I felt like I was uncaring, and I never forgave anyone, and I never loved Mom and Dad like I should have.

Then it got worse. I felt like no one loved or even cared about me. I felt like we had come all this way, and were lost, and there would be no one who would ever find us, and we were going to die here inside this stupid cave.

Jerry was struggling in front of me, and I thought he had lost his balance. He let go for a second and cried out, "No! You won't hurt us! I'll stop you!"

I finally realized what was happening. The cave was making me think this way!

"Jerry!" I cried out. "Hold on! Hold my hand again. Jerry!" I grabbed at his arm and found his hand and held on to it with both of mine.

"Winnie! What's going on?"

"I don't know. Just hold on."

At this point, Jerry fell, and I fell with him. But we didn't fall to the cave floor; we fell and skidded and slid down some kind of chute.

I screamed so loud it hurt my throat. But

Jerry was louder.

We slid down the incline and tumbled onto the floor that, thankfully, was level and we stopped rolling.

My head was spinning, but somehow, there was enough light to see. And it didn't look good. There was the stupid shaft we slid down to fall into this pit and tunnels leading in every direction.

"Oola! Where are you?" I looked up the chute we just came down, wondering if we had rolled over them.

"Humphrey?" said Jerry. He took off his backpack and looked inside. There was poor Humphrey, looking gray and dazed. I opened my pack and saw Oola in the same condition. Her eyes looked straight ahead, and she acted like she couldn't focus.

I said, "I was so worried about you. I thought we might have smushed you."

That got her attention. She shook her head a bit and looked at me. "Why did you have to say that?" She looked like she was about to cry.

Chapter 22
The Final Trial

Jerry said, "Humphrey, I hate to say it, I don't want to say it, but if I don't say it, I might just give up. So here goes: Which way now?"

That got Humphrey's attention, and he snapped out of his trance. He got to his feet, jumped down to the pit floor, walked up to the nearest tunnel entrance, and stopped.

We were in a little room with a very high ceiling. There were six openings in this room, and for the first time I noticed they were equally spaced around us. It seemed impossible that we were deep inside some scary volcano on some hidden island on some forgotten lake.

Humphrey finished inspecting each tunnel

entrance and looked at us. He was frowning. I
think maybe his little lip was trembling. "I don't
know."

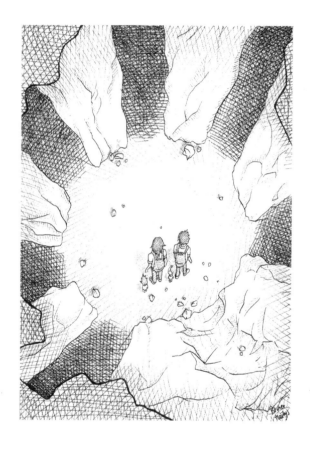

Jerry stood up. "How about this: I'll go into
one of the tunnels, and if I find something, I'll
come back and get you. If I don't find anything,
we'll try the next one."

I was astonished. I had never seen Jerry take the lead like this before. He's a brave big brother after all.

Oola and Humphrey tried to stop him. "Don't go alone, we should stick together."

Jerry said, "Well if we stick together, we'll just end up nowhere. I won't go far."

He looked at the tunnel in front of him and said, "Here I go." He stepped into the entrance, and slowly disappeared into the darkness.

I called after him, "Jerry, tell us what you see as you go."

"Okay, I'm going slowly because it's pretty dark here. I'm taking another step, feeling the walls, and... Aaaaaahhh!"

Jerry kept screaming, but it was strange, sounding everywhere at once, and then it was behind us, and he came tumbling down the shaft that we all fell from. We rushed over to see if he was all right.

Before he could say anything else, Oola jumped up.

"Stand up, everyone. Jerry, Winnie, you stand right there, back to back. Come on, stand up.

Humphrey, you stand right here, back to their sides. I'll stand on the other side."

It was very strange for Oola to run around arranging us like this, but no one protested. I mean, what else was there to do? She was acting like she knew what to do, so we did what she said.

"Let your mind go blank and think about the tunnels."

Jerry said, "Easy for me, my mind is always blank."

Oola snapped, "Stop that! You have to think about these five other passages."

I said, "What about them?"

Oola said, "Hush, and listen." She paused, and said, "One of these five is the path to the moonstones. We've traveled all these miles, taken all these falls, risked everything, and we are so close. Our moonstones are here. There is power in the stones. There is life. They are here, and we can find them."

Jerry said, "We're gonna die here."

I said, "I'm too scared to die."

"Stop it! Quiet!" We waited for Oola to

continue.

"Jerry, a minute ago, you were very brave. Is there some reason you picked that entrance?"

Just when Jerry was about to answer, Oola shushed him and looked at me.

"Winnie, you keep looking at the passage directly in front of you. Is that the way?"

"I don't know why, but it feels right."

Oola asked, "Humphrey, do you feel the power of the stones? Which way are they?"

Humphrey hesitated a bit before answering. "I was going to say that way, in front of Winnie."

Oola, moved to Jerry, "Jerry, we need to do this together. Do you feel any power, any strength coming from one of these places? Which one?"

Jerry said, "It's funny, but I almost went to the one Winnie's looking at, but I couldn't figure why one way was better than another, so…I just went the other way."

After a long pause, Oola said, "I also feel a force in that path. Come."

We picked up our packs and started towards

the tunnel that we all picked out. Humphrey and Oola walked in front, and somehow, we weren't as afraid. We should have been afraid.

Chapter 29
The Chest

Winnie's dad trudged through a forest area and came to the water known to the trolls as the Great Lake. He walked out to the beach, and to the edge of the water, and looked back at where he had been.

In one sense, he was relieved, because he calculated that even if his children had come this far, they would not go farther. Even if they had a boat, they would not go into the lake.

He looked all along the shoreline of the lake and saw the boat landings and the boat rental building to his left. Well, that would be a good place to look.

He began walking on the sand towards the building, and he wondered about this lake. He recalled seeing it on the map, but in person it was huge. It had to be some kind of reservoir, with a dam and machinery and attendants. He would ask about that later.

* * *

The tunnel led to a cave full of cobwebs, dust, and musty smells. Oola and Humphrey suddenly got all excited, "They're here! They're in here!"

There was a huge chest with a lock and chains, just like from a pirate movie. Oola and Humphrey pulled at the lock and tried to open it. Jerry whooped aloud and rushed over to help them.

I felt creepy, like there were creatures watching us from all sides of the little room. But when I looked around in the dim red light (where was that light coming from?), I couldn't see anything. Each time I moved my head, something bright and twinkly caught my eye, but when I looked back, nothing was there.

Jerry was pounding the lock with a rock he picked up, and Oola and Humphrey were trying

to undo the chains. Then I saw what no one else had noticed.

"Jerry, Oola, wait! Humphrey look at the chest lid. What is that?"

All four of us gathered to look at the lid. It first looked like some a kind of mark or picture.

"This indentation in the top is shaped like a troll," said Oola.

Jerry said, "Probably because the stones belong to the trolls."

Humphrey climbed on top of the chest to look closely at the shape. "It's exactly the shape of a troll." He sat down into the shape. "Hey, it's like a bed. I could lie down on it."

Oola said, "Oh, Hump! Be careful up there! Is that a good idea?"

Humphrey wriggled and squirmed, and then sat up again. "Well, it certainly doesn't fit me. Oh dear, maybe I've gained weight! Maybe I'm too fat!"

Oola said, "Or, maybe because it's not designed for you. Come down from there."

Jerry said, "I don't see how that will help open the chest."

I said, "Wait! It's *the one who is not one*." I pulled my Binky doll from my pocket and held it up. "It's Binky!"

Oola said, "You're right."

I didn't know what would happen, but if Binky could help get us out of here, I was willing to try. I carefully placed Binky on the image of the troll on the lid. Some blue light crackled like miniature lightning across Binky and the chains and wrapped around like ropes. There was a rumble, and the floor started shaking. The red room glowed brighter and hotter. Jerry and I were trying not to fall down. The rumble became a roar, and stones and dirt started falling from the ceiling.

There was a flash, and poor Binky exploded like a firecracker. We all screamed and jumped back. But the roar did not stop. We scrambled to the chest. There was nothing much left of Binky, just traces of purple hair now singed black.

But it worked. The lock fell open. Jerry grabbed at the chains and lifted the lid. "Come on, guys. Grab a stone and let's go."

Oola and Humphrey looked at each other wide eyed and climbed up to see into the chest. There were hundreds of moonstones. They glowed and pulsed with light. Each was a different color with its own special markings. I wanted to plunge my hands in and hold them and feel them and see what they would do.

I wanted to, that is, until the rumbling and

the shaking got worse.

"Would you guys quit shopping!" said Jerry. He coughed. "I smell sulfur."

It was getting hard to breathe. I shouted, "Come on!"

But Oola and Humphrey seemed as calm as could be. Humphrey reached in and picked up a stone.

"Look, here's my moonstone!" he said.

"Wow, here's mine, Hump!"

They were each holding a moonstone in their hands, which was great. That's why we came here. But now it looked like the end of the world.

Jerry said, "Winnie! Help me lift this thing and we'll try to get it out." He closed the lid, and together we could barely lift up the chest. We tried to carry it back to the little maze room, but we had to stop. It was just too heavy.

Oola and Humphrey acted like nothing was wrong. They weren't helping us at all.

Humphrey said, "Oolie, do you know how to use your moonstone?"

"I think so, Hump."

The room was getting hot, and there was bright red light everywhere. Little rivers of lava were flowing from small cracks in the wall. Gems in the earthen walls picked up the light and made a shiny sparkle, more and more as the lava flowed. It would have been beautiful if I wasn't so scared.

I shouted, "We are going to burn up if we don't get out of here in a hurry!"

Those two trolls just stood there looking at each other.

Oola said, "Ready, Hump?"

"Ready."

Then they held their moonstones out in front of them. The dust from the shaking got so bad, Jerry and I started coughing and had to close our eyes.

Chapter 24
The Return

When I opened my eyes, I was no longer in the smoky red room. I was on that tiny beach, and the boat was right there in front of me. Jerry, Oola, and Humphrey were there. Even the moonstone chest was with us.

That was a really strange feeling – to be one place, and then instantly, without doing anything, to be in another place.

Of course, this other place was a scary beach with a giant volcano trembling five feet away. All of us suddenly acted like well-trained Navy Seals. Jerry grabbed one end of the chest, and I grabbed the other, and we practically threw it into the little boat as Oola and Humphrey jumped in. We dragged the boat to the water, jumped in, and paddled as if, well, as if a volcano were about to explode right behind us.

And it did. I glanced back (not a good idea) and saw a giant chunk of rock fall from the mountain onto the little beach we just left. When it hit the water, this giant wave hit our boat and pushed us along faster than anyone could ever paddle. So fast that we were at the giant whirlpool again before we knew it.

Oola cried, "Oh no, not again!" but round and round we went, down the drain. I can't figure out how that all worked–we went down a whirlpool to get into this strange place, here's another one.

Through some kind of troll magic, we ended up at the pier where we stole, I mean, borrowed the little yellow canoe. As we got closer, we heard something from the shore. It sounded like a creature in trouble, crying out and screeching. Whatever it was, we couldn't see it right away. It was hidden just beyond the trees farther up the shoreline.

We had just bumped up against the dock, and Jerry and Humphrey were getting the boat secured with the little rope, when I heard a bear growl and that sound again, more like screaming this time.

Suddenly, Dad burst from the trees into the shore area, yelling and running as if he were being chased. I don't even think he saw us yet. And right behind him, I saw a bear chasing him.

"Dad! Dad!" I yelled as loud as I could and jumped out of the boat. I reached down and snatched up Oola in my hands, "Come on!"

Dad must have rounded a tree or something to get past the bear, and he was now headed back towards us on the path. And not far behind him was Moby the bear. The same mother bear as before.

Dad came up, saw us, and he panicked even more. "Get back! It's that bear and she's really mad! Run!" But he didn't wait to see if I ran; he just kept going past me.

The bear was headed right for me, and every muscle in my body wanted to run the other way. But somehow, I stood absolutely still, holding Oola out in front of me. Jerry and Dad were behind me somewhere, yelling for me to run, or duck, or play dead. But I stood still, except for the shaking of my legs.

The bear came close enough to me now that I should have been eaten up in one gulp. I looked her right in the eyes.

"MOBY! STOP!" I yelled at the top of my lungs. Not a scream or a cry, but a firm, commanding tone that I've heard my Dad give as a Dallas policeman before.

The bear stopped. It actually came to a halt, right in front of me. I knew it was Oola doing it, but it felt so good.

"MOBY! GO HOME!" I yelled again. The bear sniffed and growled at me. I could tell she was not happy.

"NOW!" That's one I've heard from Dad AND Mom in the past. Moby gave a good look past me at Dad and Jerry, snorted, and then turned and loped into the forest.

I was so excited, I put my arms close to me and held Oola close to my chest and said, "Oola, thanks! You did it! You made Moby leave us alone."

Oola had a very strange look on her face. She said, "Winnie, I was too scared. I closed my eyes, like this." And she held her hands in front of her eyes. "You did that. You made Moby leave."

Dad and Jerry came up to me. They both started yelling and patting me on the back and shaking me.

"Winnie! You faced down the bear! You could have been killed! You were awesome!"

They may have said a lot of other things, but I was not listening. I just kind of went black. They tell me I fainted.

When I woke up, there was this wind blowing in my face, and a roar. I opened my eyes just a tiny bit to see what was going on. It was a drone hovering over me (Jerry told me later they are called quadcopters, and it was part of the Ranger station search and recovery).

Dad and Jerry were standing over me, and then the drone took off. I sat up.

Dad said, "Winnie, take it easy. Just sit a while."

Jerry said, "Oh, man, Win, you fainted; just flopped down like empty clothes."

Dad said, "OK, Jerry, don't make her feel badly."

I noticed Dad's clothes then. They were all shredded and torn, and he was really filthy. It looked like most of the buttons on his uniform shirt were missing.

"Dad," I said. "What happened to you? You're

a mess."

I expected him to be kind of chagrinned and embarrassed, but he got angry, and gave us that look.

"You two are in big trouble. I can't believe what you did. You took off from the campsite this morning, and I spent the whole day looking for you. I searched this entire forest ten times over looking for you. I called the park rangers on the CB radio the moment I found you gone. I ran my car into quicksand, and I fell into the big pond, and got chased by Ol' Blue, and even got chased by that bear."

Jerry said, "I can't believe what we did, either, Dad. There was this terrible whirlpool that sucked us down, and we found an island, then there were these caves, and this exploding volcano."

I just looked at Jerry with a look I hoped would say, "Shut up!" But I didn't need to say anything. Dad looked at Jerry with this clueless expression, and he did something totally unexpected. He laughed.

"Oh yeah! Right. Exploding volcanoes." And

Dad laughed, and Jerry laughed, and I laughed. It sounded so funny when he just said it like that.

I got caught up in the story. "It's true, Dad. And the trolls helped us." Oops didn't mean to bring them up.

That's when Dad really lost it. "Oh, too much. The little trolls just waved their magic wands and..."

"Moonstones, Dad. They're called Moonstones," said Jerry.

Dad kept laughing, but I saw Jerry differently from then on. He was more than just my annoying older brother.

But then I realized I couldn't see Oola and Humphrey. "Jerry, where are they?"

Jerry said, "Who?"

"You know." I looked at Dad who was still enjoying the exploding volcano story. "The T-R-O-L-L-S." That started Dad snickering all over again.

Jerry suddenly understood. "Well, Winnie, I guess your dolls are all back at the campsite, right?" He said it real loud, nodding obviously, but looking at me funny. I picked up my backpack to see if Oola was hiding in it, but she wasn't.

I said, "Jerry, where's the... thing..." hoping Jerry knew I was talking about the chest, "...that was in the boat?"

Dad got stern again. "The very idea of you taking a boat without permission. What were you thinking?"

Jerry said, "I know, Dad. I replaced it in the same exact spot and we can pay them back."

Finally, Dad got tired of laughing at us not making any sense. "Oh, man, am I sore. Every muscle in my legs and arms is aching. I have to stretch." He began to walk around the shore out of hearing.

I said to Jerry, "OK, where's the chest, and where are the trolls?"

Jerry said, "While Dad was fussing over you, I saw Oola and Humphrey near the chest, and you know what? Next time I looked, they were gone. No footprints leading away, no heavy chest dragging marks, just poof. I think they used their magic to go home."

"Jerry, that means we did it. We helped the trolls find their moonstones!" Then it hit me. There was an empty feeling in the pit of my stomach. "But it means we'll probably never see them again."

"Well, maybe that's a good thing, Win. I don't think humans and trolls are supposed to be together. They live in a very different world than we do."

I thought Jerry was unusually philosophical, but he probably wasn't wrong. We helped the trolls. I lost Binky again, but it was okay, because it was for the best in the end.

On the way home, in the Ranger's Jeep, Dad looked at us from the front passenger's seat. "Well, you're safe now. And if you ever pull a stunt like that again. . ." Then he stopped and smiled. "It's about time you two started getting along well."

Jerry and I realized that we were holding hands. He immediately dropped mine. "Ooh, get away."

I played along. "Ooh, you were touching me."

"Keep on your side, brainless."

"Cooties! Cooties!"

"You should talk, dandruff store."

"Worm face."

"Mutant."

Dad got exasperated. "All right, knock it off. I'm sorry I mentioned it. You don't have to fight all the time, you know."

Jerry said under his breath, just so I could hear. "Softie."

I said, "Troll-lover."

That got him laughing, and I laughed too.

Chapter 25
The Trolls in Mayfield Rejoice

Asa had great confidence in the two trolls she sent. But now she fidgeted with cups and saucers on the kitchen table, and rearranged flowers on end tables for no reason. She looked out the window of her hut about every minute. Sometimes she even went to the front door and stepped out to see if anything, or anyone, was coming by.

She began thinking she acted too hastily, without consulting the mayor or even her own mother. But all that was a waste of worry; it was done.

Suddenly she heard a scraping, and a thump outside her hut. She rushed out and found Oola and Humphrey there, smiling troll-ear to troll-ear, with a large chest between them.

With a dramatic flair they flung open the chest and cried, "Ta Daa!" The moonstones shone, sparkled, and glistened like fire from inside. They both started talking at once.

Oola started, "We did it!"

"We followed the stream…"

"And came to the lake…"

Humphrey cut in. "But the whirlpool was terrible…"

"And then in the cave with the evil voices and the maze…"

"And then the exploding…"

They looked at each other and laughed.

Asa's eyes shone as she laughed and hugged her chosen trolls.

Oola said, "Come on! Your moonstone is here!"

Humphrey looked into the chest. "Somewhere in here. I'm not sure which one…"

Asa didn't reach into the chest as they expected. Instead, she went back into the hut and came out a moment later, arm in arm, with

Aerona.

The two younger trolls had not seen Asa's mother in a long time, so they had not realized how frail she had become. Asa didn't let go of her but did relax a bit as Aerona stooped down and picked up a moonstone. She straightened up, gazed at her stone a moment, then lifted it high above her head. There seemed to be a singing sound from it, and the young trolls gasped. Aerona didn't seem as old as she had just a few minutes earlier.

Next Asa picked up her stone and gave a broad smile. "Did you know that each moonstone has a special power unique to the troll's owner?"

Oola and Humphrey looked at each other, then looked at the stone in their hands.

Oola said, "How do we know? Does each stone do only one thing?"

Asa said, "The stones have powers, but each one gives the troll a very special gift. Have you used your stone yet?"

Humphrey said, "We were in the exploding volcano cave..."

Asa gasped. "Oh my!"

Oola said quickly, "It was in that maze we went through."

Humphrey said, "And Oola and I both wished we were back on the shore near our boat. And then we were."

Oola said, "Is that a special power?"

Asa said, "Watch." Then she held her stone, looked around at the little troll huts and pathways, and said, "Now."

Flowers began to bud and bloom all along the pathway from the center of town to her front door. Where the path was dusty and bare before, it became lush and green before their eyes.

Oola said, "Wow."

Humphrey said, "Can mine do that?

Asa said, "You will need to take time to discover what your own moonstone can do. For now, just use it carefully to do good for someone. You obviously know how to do that already." And she smiled a warm smile at both of them.

Asa called out to two strong trolls nearby. "Brutus! Magnum! Come quickly!"

* * *

There had never been such a spontaneous parade of joy and merriment in all trolldom. Everyone heard the shouts and joined the parade, led by Oola, Humphrey, Asa, Brutus and Magnum, each of whom had their own stones now. They carried the chest with care to the center of Mayfield and placed it on a tree trunk that could be seen by the crowd.

Mayor Omudu rejoiced that Oola was still alive, and the trolls' moonstones were found. As he gazed into the open chest, the crowd became still and hushed. Each troll strained to see what the Mayor would do. Then, with a surprised look and a smile, Mayor Omudu reached in and picked up his own stone. The crowd cheered and clapped. The Mayor enjoyed his moment of triumph as much as if it were his own doing. He then called for quiet.

"This is a grand and auspicious occasion and it behooves me to pronounce ..."

The mayor was interrupted by several shouts. "Come on, Mayor, let's go!"

Mayor Omudu was taken aback for just a moment, and then grinned. "Of course. But first, I would be remiss if I did not declare, as I do so now declare, that this celebration will be commemorated with an annual festival, and Oola and Humphrey shall be First Citizens forever honored."

The trolls applauded and cheered. Then Oola stepped up near the Mayor and spoke loudly. "I have something to say."

Everyone became quiet again to hear her.

"Merkle, please come forward."

"Am I in trouble?" Merkle was not accustomed to being singled out.

Oola laughed. "No, you are vindicated! Our journey to restore the moonstones was successful because of two humans!"

The crowd gasped and Merkle looked around in wonder.

Oola continued. "That's right. Two human children, Winnie and Jerry, went with us through every danger to find the moonstones and return. So, who in Mayfield thought humans were real? It was Merkle!"

The crowd laughed and cheered.

Mayor Omudu said, "Then the humans shall be honorary citizens of Mayfield, and we shall not fear them!"

The crowd did not cheer this pronouncement. Someone said, "Just don't bring them to Mayfield!" The crowd murmured its agreement.

The Mayor finally announced, "Form a line here and step forward to claim your moonstones!"

Merkle was nearest the chest, so he was first to find his. "My very own moonstone. How it sparkles and shines, purple and golden, flecks of green. I will always speak exultantly of you, Oola and Humphrey, Winnie and Jerry." Then he frowned a thoughtful look. "Say, Humphrey, what happened to that sacrilege?"

Humphrey replied, "That is the amazing part, Merkle. The sacrilege is what opened the chest. It was Winnie's doll, her very special doll, that she named Binky. She sacrificed her doll to help release the spell on the stones."

Merkle then stepped aside so the next troll could reach in and find her moonstone. He continued talking, to Oola, Humphrey, anyone, everyone, and no one. "Well, I didn't know that a sacrilege could be used to reclaim the moonstones. When Asa and the Mayor said it was a sacrilege, I thought that was the end of that. And then they threw it over the waterfall and it was supposed to be gone forever. And we thought Oola was gone forever, but then Humphrey said it broke the spell on the moonstones. I wonder how they knew that they needed the sacrilege to find the moonstones. And Humphrey said it had a name; Binky. Whoever heard of a sacrilege with a name like Binky?"

Chapter 26
Salutes

The Rangers dropped us off at the campsite. They pulled Dad's SUV out of the muck, and they had a repair truck clean out and restore the SUV. The Rangers said there was no quicksand in the park. I guess Dad was just exaggerating the story for our benefit.

I kept thinking about Oola and Humphrey, and if they were all right.

I whispered to Jerry. "Have you seen any sign of trolls?"

Just then, a single marshmallow fell down at our feet. We looked up and saw Oola and Humphrey waving at us from a tree limb. Humphrey waved so big he lost his balance and almost fell off the branch, and almost took Oola with him.

I looked at Jerry and said, "Trolls do not belong in trees."

He laughed.

We looked over at Dad. He was busy tying something on the car, so we walked around to where he couldn't see us talking to the trolls. They came down the tree to a lower branch to talk to us.

I was so excited to see them again. "Hey, you guys!"

Jerry said, "Where did you go?"

Oola said, "We couldn't wait to bring the moonstones back to our town. Everyone in Mayfield now has a moonstone."

Humphrey laughed, "Now I can do magic. Watch."

Humphrey raised his stone, but Oola stopped him. "Hump, don't even think about it. We aren't going to impress these two – they're Winnie and Jerry." Then she said to us, "You two are our heroes. You'll be in troll legend forever. And there are some trolls here to thank you."

Out of the quiet we could hear the sound of a hundred tiny feet stomping on the ground in unison. A parade of trolls marched by, with Asa leading the way. In single file the whole troll village came, displaying every color of hair and clothing. It was amazing, and it was just for us. They came out from under one bush just long enough to be visible, waved, and ducked under the next bush.

The parade finally ended, and Asa came back from the long line. The magic must be working because she already looked younger.

Asa said, "The trolls of Mayfield wish you good fortune and long life, Winnie and Jerry. Mayor has pronounced you honorary citizens"

Asa, Oola, and Humphrey let us rub their hair for luck, then they scampered away into the brush. I figured I'd never see them again.

Dad finally got the SUV loaded, and we climbed in.

Dad said, "Well, you two, I guess you never want to see this place again!"

I said, "Yes we do, Dad. We want to come back every year. Can we, please?"

Jerry thought about it a minute, and said, "Yeah, we want to come back. Maybe we'll catch Ol' Blue."

That was good enough reason for my Dad. "OK, son, we'll get some new rods and reels and stronger line. We'll be ready for him next time." Dad looked at me and said, "But Winnie, let's avoid the wild bears next time."

For the rest of the long ride home Jerry had

to listen to my Dad brag on every fishing trip he ever took, every time he got a new rod and reel, and every fish that got away.

I took a nap and dreamed about trolls and magic. That wouldn't have happened without Binky.

The End
(Of the first adventure)

About the Authors

The writing team of J P Coman consists of a married couple who have raised three children and use their experiences to create characters and situations that people can identify with.

J is past president of the West Texas Writers of Midland, Texas, and has been the editor for multiple Texas and Louisiana newsletters. He began writing at the age of 6 and has written poetry, comic strips, stories, puppet theater, plays, screenplays, and now his second book. Among his many interests are music, videography, theater, TED talks, Catholic bible studies, science fiction, and enjoying audiobooks.

He is married to P, the co-author of the Troll story. Her interests include church ministry, pediatric physical therapy, spiritual writing, inspirational talks, and gourmet and Cajun cooking.

They both enjoy camping, cruising, and outdoor grilling. And apparently his dishwashing skills are beyond compare.

Meet the Illustrator

Maïlys Pitcher has always been passionate about drawing and story-telling. She grew up in a bilingual family of artists, surrounded by illustrated books, paintings and French comic books, and soon knew she wanted to make art her career. In high school, she won a national drawing contest and illustrated her first children book. Since then she has done more illustrations jobs, worked on art commissions and various designing projects. She is currently studying CG animation at Mopa in France.

In her art, she wants to tell a story and engender emotions to the viewer. Lighting and colours are her favorite part of research, and she is fascinated by how they can affect and give a mood to a piece. In her spare time, she mainly enjoys walks, playing guitar, cycle rides, sketching with friends, baking, and cooking while video chatting with her family.

Learn more about her and her art at

HTTPS://MAILYSPITCHER.WIXSITE.COM/MYART

Coming Soon!

When they leave the forest in search of help, trolls bring nothing but trouble for Winnie and anyone else they come across!

Winnie and the Trouble with Trolls

Fall 2020

Find us on
humansandtrolls

Sign up at
Crimson Dragon Publishing
for news, sneak peeks,
giveaways, and more!

HTTPS://CRIMSONDRAGONPUBLISHING.COM